THE DONOR

Just after her sixteenth birthday, Will's daughter, Georgie, suffers kidney failure. She needs a transplant, but her type is rare. Will, a single dad who's given up everything to raise his twin girls, offers to be a donor. Then his other daughter, Kay, gets sick. She's just as precious, her kidney type just as rare. Time is critical, and Will has to make a decision. Should he try to buy a kidney? Should he save just one child? If so, which one? Should he sacrifice himself? Or is there a fourth solution — one so terrible it has never even crossed his mind?

Books by Helen FitzGerald
Published by The House of Ulverscroft:

DEAD LOVELY

Helen FitzGerald is one of thirteen children and grew up in Victoria, Australia. She now lives in Glasgow with her husband and two children. Helen worked as a parole officer and social worker for over ten years. Her first novel, *Dead Lovely*, is also available from Ulverscroft.

HELEN FITZGERALD

THE DONOR

Complete and Unabridged

ULVERSCROFT
Leicester

First published in Great Britain in 2011 by
Faber and Faber Limited
London

First Large Print Edition
published 2013
by arrangement with
Faber and Faber Limited
London

British Library CIP Data

FitzGerald, Helen, *1966 –*
The donor.
1. Fathers and daughters- -Fiction. 2. Twins- -Fiction.
3. Kidneys- -Transplantation- -Fiction. 4. Donation
of organs, tissues, etc.- -Fiction. 5. Large type books.
I. Title
823.9′2–dc23

ISBN 978–1–4448–1387–6

Published by
F. A. Thorpe (Publishing)
Anstey, Leicestershire

Set by Words & Graphics Ltd.
Anstey, Leicestershire
Printed and bound in Great Britain by
T. J. International Ltd., Padstow, Cornwall

This book is printed on acid-free paper

FOR MY SIBLINGS: Mary-Rose, Patrick, Brian, Michael, Peter, Catherine, Bernadette, Gabrielle, Anthony, Elizabeth, Angela and Ria
(sorry if I've forgotten anyone)

1

It was very good news. Someone had just died.

'Get to the hospital as fast as you can,' the doctor said and I asked the driver to get a move on . . . Oh God, hurry! I'd waited and waited for the call. I'd stared at my hospital-only phone for what seemed like forever, wondering what I'd feel like when it finally rang. I'd jumped every time I realised I'd forgotten to charge it, or that I'd left it on the hall table before heading out; every time another phone rang or a nearby siren blared.

I always knew my resurrection would mean someone else's death. So how could I have prayed for it? How could I have stroked my special phone, begging it to ring: *Please, just ring, for me?* How could I have spent every moment waiting for someone to die, probably suddenly, probably horribly?

As the car approached the hospital, I told myself this death was not my fault; this gift not one I could refuse. I imagined the dead man being cut into, a bit of him being taken out, placed in one of those silver padded boxes and rushed away in someone's hand, like a packed lunch of ham sandwiches.

My breath quickened. My hands trembled. It was happening. It was really happening.

Because someone was dead.

Well, not just *someone* . . .

My father.

2

Sitting under the trickle of an electric shower, Will stopped scrubbing and closed his eyes. He'd clawed at his arms for so long that new blood had now joined the red he'd been trying to wash off. He muttered to himself through the spray . . . 'I've *done* something. At last.' He slid down and lay on the cold enamel of the empty bath. He smiled. He had saved his daughters. They could go to the hospital now and reclaim their lives.

All he had to do was wait. The blood was all gone now. He'd wait and while he was waiting he'd think about where it all started.

The Bothy.

Eighteen years ago.

★ ★ ★

There was a girl on stage singing her band's latest offering, 'Wolf Whistle'. Her voice was deep and unusual, the song an angry anthem which seemed to be aimed at all men. Her black dress was so short that her panties were visible. He had a drink in each hand because Si, his best mate, had bought in bulk to avoid queues, and Will couldn't decide which one to start with. The beer on the right? Or the cider on the left? He liked both equally, but in different ways. He looked at the beer . . .

Pick me. I'm a bit bitter. I've got bite. You won't forget me.

The girl on stage had blue eyes and black hair as large as her voice. She must have seen Will scrutinising her crotch because as soon as he looked up she touched it and winked at him. He was the kind of guy to get embarrassed when caught ogling crotches. He put his head down, gazed at his feet. Something halfway there was bigger than it had been.

Despite Si's concerns, the crowd was small. Only about forty people. Will covered his own crotch with the glass of cider so none of them would notice. When he looked up at the stage, she winked at him again. She was older than Will — thirty-five or so — as bright and *other* as passion-fruit pulp. She sang a line directly at him — *Your whistle pet, is the closest you'll get.* Her head was kind of hanging down a bit, her eyes Diana-esque, looking into his.

He hadn't taken a sip of either drink. He lifted the cider and contemplated it.

Me! Me! I'm sweet. Easy. You won't even notice me.

4

The song was over and before Will knew it he was putting his untouched drinks down on the bar because the girl was heading straight for him.

'What's your name?' she said.

'Will Marion,' he answered.

'You're pretty. What do you do?'

'It's a long story.'

'Then don't tell me . . . Want to come backstage?'

'Like a groupie?' he asked.

'Yes.'

Will was twenty-nine years old. He'd only had sex with two women: Jennifer Gleeson — who'd asked him to please stop poking at her pubic bone and go get some biology lessons, and Rebecca McDonald, who'd chucked him three months before the gig. They'd been together seven years. He wasn't expecting it. 'You're a stoner,' she said. 'You do nothing and I've come to hate the very sight of you.'

This woman, Cynthia, would eventually be his third. Sober as a bastard, Will found himself sitting on a very high and wobbly wooden stool in a grotty backstage dressing room, listening as she sang the song again, just for him. She lit a joint when she'd finished (the song wasn't better the second time), drew on it for over three seconds, then asked him if he wanted to kiss her or would he rather she kissed him.

Will was a good man. As a kid he never bullied anyone, or cheated in tests, or ran away from home or told his father he was a stuck-up arsehole. Later in life, he never got into trouble with the police or broke a woman's heart. So he was good, see, but he wasn't decisive.

'Does it make a difference?' he asked.

'Yes,' she answered.

'Then you decide,' Will suggested.

'You kiss me.'

So he did.

An indecisive man needs a decisive woman.

Cynthia told Will to work hard, because if he worked hard, he was sure to be the next Steven Spielberg. He did for a while, and she brought him strong tea and smiled as he scribbled notes for a screenplay in his office.

Cynthia told Will to follow her guidance. If he did, he would be a champion lover in no time at all. Many hours were spent in bed in the first year or so. Cynthia said Will was a very quick learner. Will said Cynthia's skin drove him wild with desire.

She told him to take care of her, to cook for her, to massage her back. If he did, she would be the content and normal person she had never managed to be. The meals were regular and delicious, the massages calming and loving.

A while later, she told him to take the job with his father's holiday letting business. Perhaps hard work wasn't enough. His writing and directing projects had come to nothing.

She told him she wasn't hungry so much any more, that regular meals just represented *more* rules, and that perhaps he was using too much baby oil during the massages.

She told him she'd take care of the contraception . . .

And that the twins should be named Georgie and Kay.

Cynthia told Will to keep an eye on the kids while she went out to the shops.

★   ★   ★

Will was thirty-three when Cynthia went out to the shops. It was a Saturday morning. Georgie, three years old by then, was screaming because she wanted to go with her mum and get a lollipop. Kay was asleep, oblivious as usual to the tantrums of her sister. When Kay woke up, they waited by the window to wave when Cynthia walked towards the front door.

If she had walked towards the front door

she'd have seen a picture-postcard happy family. Loving partner: smiling. Feisty three-year-old: banging glass. Gorgeous three-year-old: chuckling.

But she didn't. At 1 p.m. Will phoned her mobile (which she'd left in the house). By 2 p.m. he'd pushed the double buggy to Cynthia's friend's house; she lived two streets down and liked the odd snort.

'Ah, she didn't come back?' Janet said. 'Ah.'

Janet was bohemian, which meant her flat was a pigsty, her hair was all over the place and her expressive butternut squash-sized breasts were dangerously unharnessed. With her toddler gnawing at the bottom of her T-shirt dress, Janet told him what she knew.

Cynthia was sick and tired of him.

Cynthia never asked to be a mother.

She was trapped.

Using again.

She wanted to be famous!

She'd emptied what there was in the accounts.

Bagged Will's expensive filming equipment.

And taken off with Heath.

★ ★ ★

Ah, Heath. He and Cynthia were like brother and sister — same foster parents as disenfranchised teens, same angry band as young adults, same love of drugs and free expression.

Will first met him about a year after he and Cynthia got together. Fresh out of jail, he arrived on the doorstep, drunk and with a bleeding cut on his cheekbone. He hugged Cynthia and said, 'Well, if it isn't Mrs Marion! It's been too long.' He patted Will's back hard enough to dislodge food, and said, 'So you're Mr Cynthia? How 'bout we all have a beer, eh?'

The three of them sat around the kitchen table while Heath described his latest adventure — his celebratory first night of freedom — which involved a baseball bat and five other men. Will laughed nervously. He'd never known anyone so scary in all of his life. If he ran out of beer, would Heath smash his head in with a baseball bat? Was the baseball bat in the large black bin liner he had with him?

'He's my brother, really,' Cynthia told Will afterwards. 'My only family. I know he's different, from a different world, but can you try to get on, for my sake, please?'

Will tried. When Heath rang the doorbell at three in the morning a month later, huffing from a scuffle, wanting the sofa and the television and a bit of a chat with his best friend in the world, he smiled and said he might get a bit of shut-eye and leave them to it.

When he and Cynthia started the band again, heading out all weekend to wow crowds of around fifteen, he smiled and said he was glad she was doing something she loved.

He tried to get on with him, but he only ever managed to fear him. Heath was a thug. He was volatile. He was dangerous.

And now, his wife had taken off with him.

How could she? Wouldn't it be like incest, if they were brother and sister really? Wouldn't she be scared all the time? Worried all the time? If Cynthia wanted to be with this guy, this brute, then who on earth was she? Certainly not the woman he cooked for and massaged, not the one whose soft skin made him wild with desire.

Will's parents and Si had tried to warn him.

'Are you sure about this?' his mum had asked when they moved in together.

'She's too . . . different,' his dad had said.

'She's a junkie nutjob,' Si had said. 'What the fuck do you think you're doin', man?'

They were all spot on. Cynthia belonged with Heath. Why he ever thought they'd work out in the long term, he'd never know. If he'd been more decisive he'd have said no to her stupid ideas — boring job, premature parenthood. If he was more decisive, he'd have realised that his attraction to her was based on awe and sex. She was like a weird bright outfit bought on holiday. She should never have been worn back home.

But he loved her. She was the artist he wanted to be. She sang in pubs with Heath and her mates, whereas Will — since completing a degree in Visual Arts — had directed nothing except the most basic of dinners. When they met Will was unemployed and living with his parents. The three film projects he'd started at uni had been in development hell ever since. He'd had good ideas, grand plans, but he rarely made it beyond the list-of-things-to-do stage. If he did ever actually write a treatment or a screenplay — and someone else offered an opinion (a writer, a producer, a financier) — he doubted himself, allowed the original idea to change and change, taking on board everyone's concerns, moving it, ruining it, going round and round in circles.

He was beginning to realise that his entire life was one long, tortuous development hell. Going nowhere. All he really did was watch movies, drink wine, listen to music, and eat crisps like a seventeen-year-old.

During their time together he had done everything to keep Cynthia around him, as if her very presence would inject him with something interesting, because God knows there was nothing interesting about him.

He understood why she went for him to begin with. He was young and allegedly good looking, and he promised he'd make her rich and famous. His initial step would be to produce an amazing music video. In their first year together he made several attempts at shooting and cutting the video, but he never quite finished it. Alcohol-inspired ideas, which he scribbled on scraps of paper as he sat on the sofa bed in his office at night, never quite materialised on film the next day. The Cynthia project ended up in messy piles in his office along with most of the others he'd ever started, until one day, she decided to do it herself. She set up the camera and sang to it. She went out and about with her band-member mates. She edited it at night using his expensive software. She filmed Will, too, to check things were working, she said.

* * *

She didn't even leave a note.

'Back soon,' she'd said, grabbing her patchwork baba bag and skipping out the door. He was sure she was skipping.

Si came around that night. He still lived in Edinburgh, an hour's drive from Will's Glasgow house. They'd lost touch for a couple of years while Will changed nappies and tried to please Cynthia. 'What a bitch!' Si said. 'What a fucking bitch.' He gave Will too much beer, advised him to track her down and kill her and left to go home and sleep for eight hours. Unlike Will, who only managed about two hours' shut-eye in total because Georgie kept waking up and asking, 'Where's Mummy?'

Bloody good question.

*   *   *

Why didn't Will try and find her? Why didn't he pull out all the stops, get off his backside and beg her to come back? He knew why now. He might even have known then but he dulled the truth with wine and soppy music. The reason was this: Will Marion was a useless lazy idiot fuckwit. He always had been. His father was right. When Will got his report cards each year, his father would say, 'Is there anything you're good at, boy?' When Will's girlfriends chucked him they both said something like, 'You're going nowhere, Will.' When Will's film projects evaporated, Si said,

13

'What do you expect, mate? You didn't even try.'

Why didn't he? Why didn't he study hard at school, work harder at relationships, work harder at work? The easy answer was that he couldn't be arsed. The hard answer was that he couldn't be arsed because he was certain he would fail.

So instead of failing to find her and failing to persuade her to come back, Will made excuses. Practical ones like babysitting. His parents wouldn't help him if he asked them, would they? They were glad to see the back of her. No point asking them to take the kids for a few days while he retraced her steps. They were the kind of grandparents who liked to tell their friends how superior their grandchildren were but had bugger all to do with them. They'd babysat once by the time Cynthia left, and only for about an hour. So there was no point, was there? And he didn't ask Si because he made both kids cry just by entering the room. He didn't ask Janet, or pay someone, convincing himself that it was the *Why* that stopped him looking for her.

What good would it have done to find her? She had another lover. She was using heroin. And deep inside, helped by the wine Will drank after the kids went to bed, he understood her reasons and admired her for it. She was better than him. She had to leave.

Confirmation of this arrived in the post two weeks after she left. It was a videotape from Cynthia. She'd scribbled on top: 'I had no choice'. Will made Georgie cry by ripping *Pingu* from the video player, inserting his wife's tape, and pressing play.

Snapshots of him, roughly edited.

The bathroom door is open. Will is taking a morning piss. From a slightly hairy bum he squeezes a fart, as he usually does, interrupting the flow only slightly.

He's channel flicking. The babies are crying but he doesn't seem to notice. His mouth is half open. There's a curry stain on his T-shirt. His blond hair's not as thick as it was but it still manages to stick up, in all directions. There's stubble on his face. He needs Botox on his forehead. He needs a bath.

He's chopping onions and it's taking him a long time.

He's snoring in bed. The covers don't cover his alcohol-induced belly.

He's saying, 'Hello, gorgeous!'

'What do you love about me?' she's asking from behind the lens.

'Um . . . ' he says. 'Everything.'

'No, what, exactly, specifically?' she asks.

15

'All of you. You're great,' he says.

He's turning the music down, then up a bit, then down a bit.

He's reading the arts section then nodding at it, then shaking his head at it.

He's stacking the dishwasher and it's taking him a long time.

'Hello, gorgeous,' he's saying.

'Talk to me,' she says. 'Tell me something.'

'Um . . . What would you like to talk about?' he replies. 'What would you like me to tell you?'

He's choosing a shirt from the cupboard and it's taking him a long time.

Making a sandwich — ham or salami?

Farting over the toilet again.

Snoring again.

Channel flicking again.

Nodding at the paper, then shaking his head at it, again.

Ahhh! Will turned it off, replaced it with the far less irritating *Pingu*.

He understood. He would have left him if he could. He was officially the most boring, disgusting, spaced-out, dithery person on the planet. By the age of thirty-three he had become a seventy-five-year-old, and not even an interesting one with Suez Crisis stories and valuable knick-knacks and stuff.

The images made him ill to the pit of his stomach. Who was he? How could he inspire such disgust — in Cynthia, yes — but mostly in himself? He had never hated himself so fully.

Will put the girls to bed, told them a story and played the video again, then again. Stopping, rewinding and replaying the failure before him, the man with no goals, no spine, no drive, no pride, no lover, no hair gel. The man with nothing.

He cried.

She didn't even say goodbye. Couldn't she have done that? A heart-wrenching but beautiful goodbye, as tear-jerking as that song 'Time to Say Goodbye'.

He put the CD on, listened to it over and over. This is what he should have had, at least.

What an idiot he'd been to not see it, to assume that she loved him because he loved her, that stress and two glasses of wine had doped her out each evening, that she'd put deposits down for the new kitchen and bathroom they'd planned and not used the money to shoot up, that she was out filming a music video or at Pilates with Janet and not fucking Heath in his flat in Denistoun.

Fucking Heath.

3

Will's neighbourhood, a sea of red sandstone, was cut off from other neighbourhoods by three main roads and a train line. Several hundred identical 1920s terraces lined undulating leafy avenues. Each contained affluent white married couples with between one and three children who were all enrolled in the excellent local schools. Churchgoers all went to the same Church of Scotland church. Boys went to the same Scout hall, girls were badged by the same Brown Owl, suits got the same train into town, joggers carved the same four-mile route around the postcode's boundary. Why would anyone venture beyond when the supermarket, post office, off-licence, florist, park, hairdresser's and tanning salon were all within walking distance? Why go into town at night when you could dine, drink and flirt in each other's houses? So everyone knew everyone. And everyone knew everything. As such, that summer, Will was the talk of the area.

Georgie and Kay's first day of nursery arrived a week after Cynthia left. When Will was on his way back, tearfully looking over the photos he'd taken on his digital camera, a gaggle of suit-widow yummy mummies saw him approaching and synchronised a gesture of sympathy — a collective slumping of shoulders, nodding of heads, sighing. He walked past them as fast as he could, but one, with blonde curly hair, dressed in three-quarter length Lycra jogging trousers and trainers, raced after him. 'Will,' she said. 'My name's Linda.'

'Hello.'

'We've . . . I've heard about your wife . . . and I wanted you to know I'm happy to do anything I can to help.'

Can you remind me to breathe? he thought to himself. *Can you fuck off?*

'Georgie and Kay are in my Bethanay's class. Would they maybe like to come for a play after nursery? Give you a wee break?'

Georgie, as difficult as she had been that morning, did indeed want to play at Bethanay's, so that afternoon Will found himself following Linda and her Cabbage-Patch-doll daughter and mad-as-a-snake toddler to their house, which was just one block from his.

'Come in for coffee.' She wasn't asking so he couldn't say no, so he followed her through her hall (identical to his but for a larger oak table) and into her kitchen (identical to his but with the new units he thought Cynthia had ordered at Magnet). He

19

sipped coffee, wondering why on earth this woman thought it was helpful to prevent him from going home to prepare dinner and finish off his work and do the washing and pre-pack tomorrow's lunches.

Linda's husband travelled a lot. This left Linda with a super king-size bed that was usually half empty. She pointed it out to Will while giving him a detailed tour of her house (identical to his bar a two-bedroom attic conversion). But she was an optimist and thought of her bed as being half full and Will knew before he left that first afternoon that he was the one she hoped would fill the other half. 'You mustn't let yourself get lonely,' she said, for example, after pointing out the original oil painting above the super king-size bed, and then, 'Don't forget I'm here to make sure you don't get down. If there's anything, *anything*, you need . . . ' etcetera and so on.

At six thirty Will walked the girls home and told himself he must never talk to any of the mothers again, especially Linda. When he unlocked the front door, both girls began crying because they were tired and starving and over-stimulated and *Where's Mummy? Why hasn't she come home yet?*

As always, Will was honest with the kids.

He sat the two three-year-olds down and told them again that their mummy was in a place far away, and that she had an addiction problem.

'What does that mean?' Kay asked.

'It means her body tells her she needs bad things.'

'What bad things?' asked Georgie.

'They're called drugs,' he said. 'It's kind of like mummy's sick. And she doesn't feel able to see you at the moment. Maybe we should let her be. Maybe we should count our blessings.'

'Okay then, Daddy,' said little Kay.

'What's blessings?' mumbled Georgie.

Will poured himself a glass of wine, his mood mirroring the disastrous journey of the baked beans he'd put on the cooker: simmering, boiling, burning: holy crap, he couldn't even cook baked beans.

Georgie refused to eat them. 'You ruin everything! You made Mummy leave! I hate you! It's all your fault!' She pushed the bowl of blackened beans off the table. They splattered to the floor. Unremorseful, she looked at her father and said, 'You're stupid.'

She was only three, wee Georgie, but so angry and unhappy. Will had never experienced anything as sad as watching a sad child.

★　★　★

That night, Will wrote a letter.

Dear Cynthia,

Georgie and Kay started nursery today. They are beautiful little girls, but Georgie in particular is angry and she doesn't understand why you left her.

She blames me. Could you write to her? Could you send her some photos? Could you come and see her? Perhaps you could explain why she has no mother, because I can't.

Will

He never sent it, of course.

★   ★   ★

Despite Will's pledge never to speak to Linda again, the girls' busy lives necessitated constant interaction with her and the other suit-widows. He had no time for male friends. Si hadn't been in touch since Cynthia left — why would he be? Will had neither the emotional nor physical resources to play golf, drink and fuck around. Before long, he was declared to be one of the girls. But he didn't fully belong in any of the places he needed to be: ballet classes, cheese-and-wine nights at the nursery, PTA meetings. He may as well have been a little green alien. His newfound peers talked about face creams, curtains and unhelpful partners. They looked at him like they looked at their kids — *Ah, isn't he cute.* They wanted to feed him. They wanted to pat him on the head. They wanted their partners to be as good at getting out stains as he was. They wanted coffee mornings to be at his house so they could watch him at work, admiring and despising him at the same time (*Look, he's a man, and he's slicing a cake. Isn't that great? Look, he's a man, and he's slicing a cake, isn't that screwed up? Take the knife from him now! Make him a ginormous salami sandwich! Turn on the football! Offer him your body!*).

It took three months before Linda officially offered Will hers. The ballet show had run late. She came into his house on the way home (Bethanay had left her favourite teddy in the bedroom, or some such excuse) and asked for a drink.

'I'd better get the kids to sleep,' Will said.

'Put them in front of a video. They'll be asleep in two seconds.'

'Are you sure that's a good idea? They'll be knackered tomorrow.'

23

'I'm sure it's a good idea,' she said, switching on SpongeBob and pouring them both a glass of red wine.

'I love watching you with your kids,' she said. 'You put me to shame. So patient and devoted!'

'You know what I find amazing?' Will said. 'Sometimes when I think about them, or look at them, I get butterflies. Y'know that falling in love feeling? No matter how difficult they're being, or how tired I am. That's lucky, hey? To have that. I don't suppose the chemistry goes the same way as it does for lovers, does it?'

'I only get that when they're asleep,' Linda laughed, moving closer. 'You are a lovely man.'

Will closed his eyes as she kissed him, trying to immerse himself in her decision. *You are someone who likes me*, he said to himself, tongue now implicated. *You are not Cynthia. Cynthia does not exist.*

'I can't.' He pushed her away a little roughly.

'I'm sorry . . . ' She sounded annoyed.

So was Will.

It wasn't that he didn't find her attractive. Linda was a good-looking woman. She had the kind of bum men can't help but want to grab. She had smiley blue eyes. Her breasts appeared defiantly upright despite thirty-three years of bouncing and three of

24

breastfeeding. The problem was that Will was still in love with a woman he hoped — expected — would turn up one day, sorry and shamefaced and drug free and desperate to love him. This part of him stared out the window each night after the kids went to bed willing her to appear. It practised what she might say when he opened the door:

Forgive me.

How can you forgive me?

I beg you to forgive me.

Where are they? Are they sleeping?

It practised what she might write in a letter:

Dear Will,

Get me away from this man! He holds me here. I will try to escape again tomorrow.

Yours, C.

Or . . .

Dear Will,

I left to go into rehab. I couldn't face telling you how serious my problem was. But I am doing well, and I will be home soon.

Yours, C.

It practised what she might say on the phone:

I am on my way. Nothing you can say will stop me from making it up to you.

It practised opening the door, seeing her there. Being silent, then angry, then sexually aggressive, then tender, forgiving, loving, for the rest of his life.

It practised switching off from anyone or anything that might prevent this reconciliation from happening. Linda, for example, who held back after that fateful kitchen kiss, and became his friend.

'Good Guy', she called him. 'Hey, Good Guy, I'm taking you to the supermarket.'

'Good Guy, we're going walking. It doesn't matter that it's raining!'

'Come over for dinner, Good Guy.'

Dinner was the first of many bad ideas. It was the usual Saturday night in the neighbourhood. Four couples gathered in every fourth house to eat meals involving fresh coriander. In this case, there were three couples and Will.

He had to bring the kids. And, while Kay played with Archie and Bethanay upstairs, Georgie wouldn't leave Will alone. She sat on his knee throughout the four-course ordeal like a poised-to-pounce cat, not eating anything, not talking, crying, screaming, anything. It was as if she was Tasered by the coupledom — Ah, so that's what a married couple acts like, her wide eyes seemed to say as she gazed around the table.

★ ★ ★

'Your husband is very nice,' Will said to Linda the next time she saw him in the school playground.

'He is. But . . . '

'But what?' Will said.

'I dunno. Guess we've been together a long time. Kind of becomes a business, marriage, after a while. Not sure who's the managing director. And there's always the possibility of cutbacks.'

'Is he good in bed?'

Linda slapped him on the arm. 'He's a little girly, maybe.'

'What about counselling?' Will suggested.

'It's not that bad. But, yeah, can't say it hasn't crossed my mind, for the kids, like. They must sense the atmosphere's a bit strained.' Linda sighed. 'Counselling. Get everything out in the open. Is that really a good idea?'

The conversation was interrupted by Bethanay and Kay racing out of school, Georgie skulking along behind with a wad of her latest drawings in hand.

27

'Daddy!' Kay said, wrapping herself around his legs.

Without dislodging cling-on Kay, he leant down to hug Georgie. 'You scrunched my artwork, you idiot,' she said, elbowing a quick release and walking away.

4

As months turned into years, yearnings for a remorseful Cynthia faded. Will focused all his attention on the girls, hoping they would be content and happy without their mother.

Kay *was* happy. She was always happy. How could twins be so different? Both brown-eyed and blonde-haired, but on the inside, so very different. Kay came out of her mother's body with a smile on her face and it never left. Whenever Will looked at her, his blood warmed. Whenever he thought about her, he smiled. She was endorphins to him: chocolate, exercise, all things good.

On Christmas morning, Kay always ran downstairs at 6 a.m. — breathless — to shake, touch and then open her gifts. She'd jump up and down afterwards, hugging him, saying, 'You are the best daddy in the whole entire world. Thank you! I love you!' This reaction was despite the fact that Will was totally crap at gift buying (and wrapping), dilly-dallying around till the most-wanted toys were sold out and buying inappropriate alternatives instead (a basketball instead of a netball, Princess Diaries 1 instead of Princess Diaries 2). No matter what cock-up he'd made, Kay was happy. She'd laugh about it later, but never complain at the time.

On her first day at school, Kay walked into the school building, her head held high. Will wept as she disappeared inside. From then on, as he waited in the playground for the bell to ring, he would keep his eyes on the school door, unable and unwilling to join in conversations about bathroom renovations, anticipating the smile that had always stopped him moping.

'Daddy!' she would say, running towards him and grasping his legs.

'Hello, petal!' Will would say. 'How was your day?'

She'd tell him all about it on the way home. Janey was being mean (asking for private talks with her other best friend Charlotte). Mrs Jones had given her team a gold star for keeping their table tidy. Archie was in trouble again. She got nine out of ten for a maths test. She had pizza for lunch.

There was nothing complicated about her. Emotionally intelligent is what she was. She knew how she felt and why. She knew what she wanted and why. No second guessing. Even when she started her periods, she was matter of fact about it.

I'm feeling hormonal, she told her dad. *I've written what I need from the chemist on your shopping list.* And that was the end of it.

God forgive him, but Kay was the light of Will's life. Nothing about her reminded him of Cynthia. Nothing about her upset him. She didn't despise him. And he would have done anything, anything, for her.

Kay wrote an essay in fourth year. Will found it in a pile of old papers on her desk. It was called 'The Person I Admire Most'.

The person I admire most is my Dad. He's gorgeous. Obviously in a Dad-like way, but he's slim, he's still got all his thick blond hair, he wears the carefully selected clothes I buy for him, and wears them well. He doesn't smile much, except at us, but he has a kind face, an approachable face, the kind of face that makes a stranger ask for directions, or the time.

He's popular. He doesn't admit it, but all the other mums fancy him. Maybe he doesn't even know it. 'Don't be silly!' he says when I tell him what my friends have overheard their mothers saying.

He's never been on a date, not since the Mum left. I've tried to make him, but he won't go.

He's a terrible cook. He makes basic meals five times a week like pasta with sauces from those tubs in the supermarkets — five cheeses, tomato and mascarpone, carbonara — and the other two days are treat days (i.e. carry out).

He's untidy. His tiny office, especially, smells of teenage boy, with several sets of slippers, scrunched-up bits of paper, dirty coffee cups, piles of unfiled filing on the sofa bed, cameras on the floor, film posters on the wall (Psycho, Strictly Ballroom, The Mist).

He's devoted to his children. Since Mum left, he has thought about nothing but our welfare, sacrificing the film career he so wanted for a boring home-based admin job, ferrying us to swimming lessons and netball and friends' houses, going shopping for clothes and sitting next to the fitting room while we try things on.

He's broken. Lonely. Oh what I'd do to make him happy, to help him find some-thing other than us to fill his life because we'll leave one day, one way or another. We'll be gone, and all he'll have is his untidy office, his boring job, and an empty house he no longer knows how to leave because he's never had any reason other than us to leave it.

I admire him because despite all his diffi-culties he's kind and generous. He does nothing but give. And I am lucky to receive from him every single day.

Will must've read this about three thou-sand times. It always sent him to sleep with a smile.

★ ★ ★

He would often read the essay after lying in bed worrying about Georgie, who did not come out of her mother's body with a smile on her face. She screamed herself blue. Will tried to hold her after the nurse had weighed and measured and checked her, but she frightened him with her anger and he handed her back almost immediately, taking Kay instead, who'd fallen asleep after two minutes of smiling.

When they were toddlers, Georgie would follow Kay down the stairs on Christmas morning, rubbing her eyes with exhaustion. She'd relish Kay's excitement, insisting that her sister open all her presents first. 'It does feel like a teddy bear!' she'd say as Kay poked at the badly wrapped gift. 'Why don't you open it? Oh look what Daddy bought you! Yes, it is beautiful.' Eventually, she'd open hers, ripping paper quickly, discarding, moving on to the next. Will couldn't recall her showing anything other than disdain for anything he'd ever bought her. ('Why is this pink? Did you forget my favourite colour?')

While Kay had waved at Will (smiling) as she walked into school for the first time, Georgie had howled and grasped his legs and yelled. 'I don't want to go, Daddy! I want to stay home with you.' He hadn't known what to do, except to say, 'Look at your sister. She's excited. She *knows* it's gonna be fun. Why don't you follow her in?'

'Why don't *you* follow her in?' Georgie said as a teacher took her hand and led her towards the door.

After that, each afternoon as he stood in the playground with the mums, a tiny worry would niggle the back of his mind. (What would Georgie's problem be today? She had the wrong gym kit? Her teacher yelled too much?) No matter what it was, he always tried to be positive, and sometimes he managed — like the time every other girl in the class — including Kay — was invited to Mhairi Magee's soft-play birthday party. Will sat Georgie down and said it was a mistake, that Mhairi's mum said she had put an invitation in the schoolbag. 'Thank goodness she couldn't find it,' he told her. 'You can't go, because I've already booked tickets for us to go tobogganing!' But mostly, Will felt he failed to react to Georgie's worries appropriately. They seemed to seep into him and shudder.

In fourth year, Georgie also had to submit an essay about the person she admired most. She chose Gandhi. Will wasn't surprised. If she ever wrote an essay about him, he would not want to read it.

5

At least *I* left him a note.

Dad,

Don't be angry with me. I'm sixteen and I can do what I want now. I've gone to find my mum.

G

Okay, so I ran away a week before my final exams, but what did it matter? I was dumb as dog shit anyways and had no ambitions other than the one I ran away to do. Plus it was his fault. He drove me away with his lump-of-lard-ed-ness. What did he ever do? What had he ever achieved? If I'd had to come in from school one more time to find him listening to that stupid song 'Time to Say Goodbye', and eating crisps, I would have murdered him. If I'd had to eat out with him one more time and wait while he pondered the menu (*What are you having? What would you recommend? Could we share? Could you order for me?*) I would have killed him all over again.

Get this, right: he couldn't even decide where to go on holidays. Every summer, about a week before the break, he'd get us round the kitchen table and play some stupid game. He'd hide a five-pound note under his hand and say, 'Bessie up or down?' We'd take turns each year. 'Down!' Kay would say enthusiastically, and if she was right, if the noggin of England's Queen was down the way, she'd get to decide (between a caravan in Arran or a cottage in fucking Arran!). We never went anywhere else, ever. Kay and I were the only ones in our year never to have been across a bigger stretch of water than the one between Ardrossan and Brodick.

He drove *her* away too. I completely understood how she must have felt: suffocated, frustrated, angry, wanting to run for the hills screaming, 'I'm free!'

I knew he would have been angry with me. He was always angry with me. He'd have yelled, 'Why? Why me? What have I done? Have I not given you everything?' He'd have wondered why I chose *now* to leave; screwing up my education when he'd done everything he could to keep us in this decent area, in these decent schools. He'd have said to Kay, 'Have I not been good to her? Have I not spent every spare minute with her, encouraged her friendships, listened when she needed to talk, put up with her tantrums, her rage at the world?'

Poor Kay. I can imagine she would have told him it wasn't his fault. She'd have made him a cup of tea and put her arm around him and told him she loved him and that I loved him too, in my own way, and that maybe I just needed to do this thing. Maybe he should just let me.

He wasn't able to. He was worried that I'd harm myself. I'd been drinking for a few years by then, my addictive personality perhaps inherited from my drug-using mother. He probably assumed I'd get proper wellied and do myself or someone else in. So he left Kay with his groupie housewife and drove to Central Station. That's the problem with using someone else's credit cards. They can find you. Within hours of my departure, he knew where I was and what I was doing. Should've withdrawn the cash like Mum did.

I was walking along the platform when I heard his voice. I turned to see him running towards me with that dumb, tearful face. I thought about pushing my way through the crowds of people waiting at each carriage door but I didn't have the strength.

How long had it been since I'd had any strength? A long time, looking back, the first real clue being about a year earlier, when I started avoiding all stairs, taking time to consider if I really needed to ascend to my bedroom or to my locker on the second floor at school. As time wore on, my weariness grew. Maybe I needed sleep, perhaps it was that extra vodka down the park the night before, or was it that time of the month? But as weeks grew into months, one thing after another adding to my general sense of ill being, it became obvious that something might be wrong. Why did I need to pee all the time? Did the boy at the end-of-year party get me pregnant? (I did a test. He didn't, which was no surprise as his mother had walked into his bedroom before either of us managed to reach the end.) Why, when peeing was an ongoing and urgent need, did nothing come out when I made it to the loo? *Come pee, come*, I would beg. *Why on earth won't you come?* Did I have an STD? A urinary infection? I was tested for the former at the family planning clinic (all clear) and drank those powder things that get rid of the latter (didn't work). So why?

And why, when it did come out sometimes, was it like milkshake froth? Why were my ankles swollen? Why was I itchy and nauseous? Why did I have a foul taste in my mouth that no amount of toothpaste or mouthwash would get rid of? For several weeks before my attempt to find my mother, I had spent long periods each night googling online medical services, only to discover that I had every disease there is.

'You're worrying about nothing,' Kay said, when I asked her about the milkshake froth one night. 'I get that sometimes too. I'm sure it's normal. Maybe hormones? And of course you're tired. You never sleep!'

But as I stood on the platform, my father before me, I knew there was something seriously wrong, not just hormones or lack of sleep. *Ah, fuck*, I thought, breathless. I would need to talk to him.

'Georgie, please don't do this.'

'You can't stop me.'

'But where are you going? How are you going to find her?

'I'm going to see the guy she ran off with. Janet told me how to find him.'

'Where is he?' I could hear a tremor in my father's voice. A pathetic tremor that stifled his thoughts: *Why didn't I do that? Why didn't I ask Janet about Heath?*

'He's in HM Prison Manchester.'

6

To whom it may concern . . .

A ruler flattened the floor of Heath's words . . .

I am writing to ask for parole. I have changed a lot since my offence. My partner, Cynthia Marion, is in rehab. She says she is waiting for me to get out to help her achieve what I have achieved. I am very motivated to help her. Please please believe me. I am sorry for what I done and I will be law abiding from now on. The people I used to hang out with are gone from my life.

Yours faithfully,

HEATH JONES

This first letter, scribed, tongue out, three years prior to Georgie's planned visit, had come to no good. Heath hadn't expected early release, not on first application, but it pissed him off nevertheless, so much so that he phoned

41

Cynthia in rehab feeling so sorry for himself that he decided to tell her she shouldn't bother waiting for him any more (*Leave me and you'll fuckin' regret it!*) and that she should start afresh (*Bring me some gear or you'll fuckin' regret it.*)

'I'm out of here Friday,' Cynthia said. 'I'll bring something in then.'

He thought of her as his Cathy. He the dark brooding love-her-of-life Heathcliff. They had been destined for each other since they met as teenagers, never quite having fun together, but never quite aiming to either. He would never let her leave him. She would never want to.

'Cynthia,' he said. It was the only word that made him weak.

'Heath,' she replied, this being their goodbye.

★ ★ ★

The following year, Heath sat at his desk, ruler in hand, and wrote a second letter to the parole board:

Fuck you all. There is no fucking point. The guy was not a hostage. He was a fucking social worker. He came into my cell to nip my head all the time.

As usual, Heath phoned Cynthia before the ink of his rejection had dried. Mobile phones were strictly forbidden in the prison, but strictly necessary, and Heath always had the most up-to-date under his mattress. This sentence, he had an iPhone. He used it for porn. He used it for games. He used it to organise the bringing-in of drugs — he had three types of contact for this on the outside: the dealer (there were three he trusted, two of whom he'd protected during previous sentences), the person who paid the dealer the money (he left money with a friend in Manchester who was very scared of him) and the courier (which the dealer organised, who used various methods to get the gear inside, often involving the support of a corrupt officer). Heath also used the phone to organise punishment on the outside should something go wrong with the deals, arranging for so and so to be maimed by so and so. And, of course, the phone gave him easy access to the love of his life. With a cell phone in his cell, he was the managing director of a fully operational business.

'Oh, Heath,' Cynthia said when he called to tell her the bad news. 'What am I supposed to do without you?'

Cynthia had visited regularly for years, but in this last year, expression had receded from her eyes each time. Her hair had become thin, dry, unwashed, unbrushed. Was he losing her? She had already lost herself.

I am sorry for taking the social worker hostage last year,

Heath wrote twelve months later.

I just wanted more visits. I didn't understand how you could take visits away just because of some random tests. I have completed another course in victim awareness and realise that the social worker must have been very scared when I wrapped him up in the sheet. I am very sorry for this because he was just trying to do his job and it's no excuse that his job is a stupid one and that he's useless at it.

Please consider me for parole. I am a changed man now. I want to stop using. I really do.

When I think of the man I killed I feel sorry now. It ruined my life.

HEATH JONES

'No,' two men and two women took turns to say from their table. 'We do not think you are ready.'

The following day, after Heath phoned with the bad news on his recently upgraded iPhone, Cynthia visited him. 'I can't wait here any longer,' she said. 'I need to get away till you get out.'

Heath was devastated, but he understood how she felt. 'I'll get out next time,' he said. 'One way or another. You will come back for me?'

'Of course I will,' she said.

★ ★ ★

The last year had been the slowest yet. In his cell, he tossed his fifth attempt at a letter to the parole board in the bin and lay down on his bed to look at the photograph he'd cherished for years. Cynthia, lying in a field. Elbow to head, not smiling at him, but loving him. 'I know you'll come back,' he said to himself. 'I know you will.'

'You know a Georgina Marion?' an officer was asking through the spy hole in his cell door.

It took Heath a few seconds to recognise the name of his beloved's daughter. 'Aye.'

'She wants to visit you. I'll add her to your list then, yeah?'

7

Finding my mother wasn't my only mission. Hers was a love story that kept me alive. I knew she'd run off with the love of her life. Janet had leaked it one afternoon in the supermarket when I was nine.

'Have you ever heard from my mother?' I asked her as she weighed courgettes. Dad was at the deli counter, so I felt safe asking. I think Janet was a bit surprised. I probably should have said hello first.

'No,' she said.

'Where did she go?'

'I don't know, honey,' she said. 'Love's a funny thing.'

'It is,' I said, not knowing what she meant, but hoping she'd think I did and tell me more. 'Is she still in love, do you think?'

'No idea. That Heath Jones is a strange one. Not sure what she sees in him. But she never was able to get him out of her system.'

After that, I fantasised about my mother's love for a strange man called Heath Jones. He was always in her system. How romantic. I wanted to see that kind of sacrifice and love first hand. And then, I wanted to find it

46

myself. Boy meets girl. Boy loses girl. Boy gets girl. Mum had found it. She'd sacrificed everything for it. I wanted it.

Four hours is a long time when your feet have swollen to the size of basketballs, when you're freezing cold and breathless and waiting for the toilet to be vacant again so you can retch into the sticky bowl. I was desperate for air, but when I staggered off the train and made my way to the taxi stand, it merely fuelled my nausea. The driver was so nervous about my physical state that he stopped three times on the way to the prison.

HM Prison Manchester, previously known as Strangeways, was the home of the quickest hanging in history — 7.5 seconds from cell to death — and had housed Britain's best-known serial killers: Moors murderer Ian Brady and the GP Harold Shipman. I'd read all about the place, imagining my mum visiting her lover there, hooking her fingers through the bars to touch his, saying, 'I will wait for you, my darling.' I imagined her writing him letters with secret messages involving symbols and code words — 'How 4are you?!' might mean, for example, 'Next visit I will smuggle in Belgian chocolate.'

It hadn't been hard to find out about Heath. All I had to do was ask Janet, who Dad couldn't stand — he said it was because she talked too much, but I knew it was because she was Mum's best friend back then. He'd blacklisted anyone who'd been onside with Mum.

'Sure I know where he is,' Janet said. 'He's been in prison for years. It was all over the papers.'

She googled his name as I looked over her shoulder. Within seconds I was staring at the big square frame of Heath Jones, my mother's lover. The picture was taken from a fair distance. He was walking out of the High Court. It was hard to make out his features exactly, but you could tell he was handsome, in an 'I might kill you any second' kind of way. Every feature scowled. His nose: flared in anger. His mouth: tense and closed and alien to smiling. Eyes: the kind newspapers love to print — pure hate, pure evil.

GLASGOW DEALER GETS LIFE,

the article beside the photograph said:

Heath Jones was sentenced to life in prison today for the murder of the infamous Glaswegian criminal Panda McTee, whom he stabbed in a lane near Queen Street Station, Glasgow,

twelve months ago. Lord Johnstone con-
cluded that Mr Jones 'showed no
remorse for his cold-blooded brutality'.
Psychiatric reports stated that Mr Jones
suffered from borderline personality dis-
order and had no victim awareness
whatsoever. His previous offences
included seven assaults, two of them
against women.

'Thanks, Janet,' I said. I went home and set about arranging a visit.

I must have fallen asleep in the taxi. When I woke, the driver was gently shaking my shoulder.

'Are we there?' I asked, unable to sit up properly. Heath Jones was expecting me at 1 p.m. Sweat was pouring from my body. I felt like I might die.

'No,' he said. 'We're at the hospital. You've been making sounds. You look bad. You need to see a doctor.'

As much as I didn't want to admit it, he was right, and I got out of the car and staggered into the A and E. It was two hours before a doctor examined me.

'You have high blood pressure,' he said. 'And there are a few other things we're worried about. We want to run some tests.'

8

And this is where Will's story began. Not sooner than this because it's not a tale about a frustrated artist, or a scorned lover, or a new man, or a struggling single father. It's a story about kidneys. Two bits of squidgy brown flesh, till now the companion of steak in his mind but from this moment on linked with the survival — or not — of his daughter. Georgie's kidneys had packed it in, the doctor said when the test results came back. They were still in Manchester, and the only words Georgie had spoken to him were, 'I'll find her as soon as I'm better.' As the doctor explained further in his depressing white hospital office, Georgie's face fell, because she realised that time might never come. She had kidney disease. Her liver was suffering. It was rare in teenagers. It was established, chronic, incurable, progressing rapidly. Georgie needed more than medication. She needed machines to sustain her for now, and a transplant to sustain her for longer. But the chances were slim, her type rare. It was a genetic disease, caused by the gross mismatch of Will and Cynthia — how many more ways could they have been mismatched? — which meant Kay was screened in Glasgow almost immediately after her sister's diagnosis.

Was Will more scared waiting to hear about Kay's result? Did he sleep less? Eat less? Tremble more?

Was he angrier when it came in? Or was it a natural reaction to the doubling of misfortune?

Did he cry more when they told him Kay would have to wait just as long?

And when he punched the door of his never-renovated kitchen, was it because both of them had rare types? Or was that jagged fist hole for Kay alone?

If bad luck comes in threes, Will felt he'd had all his.

Georgie's body was dying.

Kay's body was dying.

And he was the only probable and willing match.

Locked in the upstairs bathroom, shirt off, black marker in hand, he drew a kidney shape on his left side and another on his right.

'These are my kidneys,' he said. 'And there's only one spare.'

9

Almost as soon as I became ill, I got a new boyfriend. He presented me with a comfy armchair and I accepted. He was dull and predicable, a replica of my father. He liked to feed me but he couldn't cook. He liked to be with me but he had nothing to say. He liked to give but he always took more.

Oh gurgling machine.

I'd have liked a different kind of boyfriend. One who moved, for example. One who touched me and didn't just stick it in me and suck and drip and turn my arm to noisy lumps. But I couldn't have a different kind of boyfriend. I probably never would. What would I say? 'Not Monday, Wednesday, Friday or Sunday, Jim (for example), I'll be busy then.'

'We could have dinner after,' he might suggest, and I'd have to say, 'But where/what kind? 'Cause there's all sorts of shit I can't eat now. Like bananas. If I eat a banana I'll probably die, but then I'll probably die anyways.'

'What about a walk?'

'I'd love to, Jim, but I'm exhausted, like all the time.'

'What about we watch a movie on one of the days in between?'

'Nup. I'll be too busy drinking gallons of water and feeling like crap, and anyways I'm yellow. Do you really want a yellow girlfriend?'

Bye bye, Jim (for example).

I named my new boyfriend Alfred. He looked like an Alfred. A square white robot with wires, some very red, some less so. Sometimes I imagined him talking to me and it was always with a deep Alfred-like voice (*Now, now, Georgina, you know you should stay still.*). Alfred who sucked me out and filled me up again and would do so till I died, or till someone else died first, a very special someone, with a limited Gucci-bag-kidney like mine, the type you see in the 'Get her style' section of magazines, carried by a B-grade celeb who joined a waiting list and paid thousands to *just get that damned bag* in order to improve her standing.

It was more boring than visiting one of Dad's housewives for coffee or reading a full non-fiction book or listening to Dad read his pre-proposal for an outline of a short film. He read it to us when we were ten. Fifteen minutes had never been more excruciating. What was it about again? All I remember is a leaf. It was a not very interesting brown.

I couldn't even smoke in there. Had to use foul nicotine chewing gum that made me hiccup.

The doctor in Edinburgh gave me a leaflet when he had told me I needed Alfred. On the front of the leaflet, a woman was sitting in a chair like mine smiling happily as if it was the best place in the world to be. 'You should try this!' her smile said from the glossy page. 'You should try it now! Even if it's very expensive!' The woman was at least forty. Perhaps for her it was fun, compared with fighting face lines and ordering toilet paper in bulk. But I was sixteen. I had parties to go to, drugs to take, countries to see, love to fall in. I bet the woman on the brochure didn't even have the disease. I bet when they wrapped the photo shoot she said, 'Thanks, Maxie!' whisked the plug from her unpunctured arm and went out shopping while eating a banana. Wish they'd have asked me to pose for it. I'd have done the Vicky and then the middle finger and then the loser sign and then scowled, 'They are all liars! This is fuckin' dreadful, I hate it and so will you!'

Some say boredom enhances creativity. Sickly children go on to direct Oscar-winning films and pen Booker-winning books. I didn't give a fuck about writing books or directing films. I wanted to go down the offie and then to Club Boho. I wanted to shag someone again. Would Alfred really be the love of my life? *That's it, that's it, right there, Alfred, yes.*

There is something very unsexy about depending on someone. If I pulled him out, I'd regret it. So I wouldn't. I'd semi-decline there, four times a week, four hours a go, and be thankful for Alfred while hating the very sight of him. For most people, I supposed, this is what marriage is like.

I'd try hard not to look at Alfred, scouring the people-filled room instead. There's:

EVIE. She is fifty-two. Too old for her name. She has short bright red hair, probably a hangover from her art-teaching days. Her granddaughter bought her a portable DVD player and she watches BBC adaptations of Catherine Cookson novels on it. I can hear the dreary dark rain through her earphones.

JIMMY. He's forty. He's heard a rumour he's next to go. He rubs his phone as an expectant mother rubs her bursting nine-month belly.

PEGGY. She's very old. I don't know how old. Being here doesn't seem to worry her. Even though she knows she's never getting a new one. I expect she sits still at home in the same way. Here, at least, she has SAMUEL to talk to.

He's around thirty-eight. He gets angry when people get the call inexplicably before him. He shouts at nurses, things like: 'What is the system? How can this be? Did he use his connections? Did he *pay?*'

Samuel was talking about RON, forty-nine. He was very rich. Knew people. How come it only took three months for him to be whisked away and inserted with a red lump of life?

And, of course, there's Kay, sitting beside me, reading her books, taking notes carefully and optimistically, as if one day she will actually finish school, graduate, be a physiotherapist. As if.

★ ★ ★

'Georgie, how you feeling?' Like clockwork, my father had arrived. Looking at his eyes evoked the same feelings as looking at Alfred. So I didn't.

'Bored,' I said, staring blankly over his shoulder.

'I brought your iPod. Put some new tunes on.' He paused, sat down, fidgeted. 'Georgie, I'm going away for a few days.'

'Oh?' I didn't believe him. He sometimes made grand gestures at a change of routine (*We'll go to Ireland for the weekend . . . We never did . . . never got further than Arran*

. . . I need to get out of this job . . . Didn't. *I'm going to write a horror film, starting next week . . .* Never did . . . *Let's play badminton Thursdays, as a family . . .* Yeah, yeah).

He paused. 'I'm going to find your mother.'

I may have flinched a little, but within seconds my default 'whatever' had taken control again. Like he would get off his arse and do something meaningful. Like I didn't know him too well. He'd go home after the visit, put on the telly, drink too much wine and forget all about it.

I had a coping strategy. I wasn't going to think about any of it any more. I wasn't going to worry about my blood and how dirty it was and where it came from, and who it came from, any more. After Dad left, I decided to go out and find a boy. His name would not be Alfred.

★ ★ ★

'What colour would you say I am?' I asked a boy who went by the name of Eddie. As usual, I felt tired and nauseous, but I was on a mission.

'I dunno. Normal.'

'You're a smooth talker, Eddie.'

'Pink, then, like very nice roses.'

That was better. Eddie had a job and a flat.

I wasn't interested in either.

My attempt to fall in love with him went something like this (before I list the events, let me just tell you outright that it failed):

Eddie and I drink too much beer in a pub in the Southside then get a taxi into a club in the town, where we drink too much vodka.

Eddie dances badly, but likes the way I dance. He holds me by the hips, hooks one leg through mine and tries to rub me with the top of his quad.

Eddie says we should get out of here.

In the taxi, Eddie puts his hand under my shirt and feels my nipple. I'm so tired. I don't like having my nipples felt. Tweak tweak pinch, like ow, like why?

We arrive at his flat in Shawlands and, still determined to fall in love, I follow him up a paint-peely close and into the hall, which has three bikes in it.

What do you like about me? I ask him and he says it's my tits.

In the bedroom, Eddie undresses. He's very thin and white. I can see at least two ribs. He has either shaved his pubic hair or he's eleven. His penis looks like a nose.

What first attracted you to me? I ask him. *It was your tits,* he says, pulling my bra over my head without bothering to unclip it and catching my top lip for a moment along the way.

He pops one of what he likes about me in his mouth. I feel sick. I don't like how he's gnawing at me. What am I? A breastfeeding mother? *Unlatch*, I say, so he does, a little taken aback, before heading towards the lower region, taking my jeans and pants down, kneeling.

Am I actually going to vomit? I don't like how he's lapping at me. *When you spotted me on the dance floor did you think I was beautiful?* I ask, but his mouth is too busy to say more than *Mmm hmm.*

Eddie is very quick at what he does next. Jack rabbit bang bang bang and he's so thin I can hardly feel him on top and he sighs and slides off and says *Ah!* and lights a fag and I say *Well?* And he says *Well what?* And I say *What was it that attracted you to me?* And he says *God, haven't we done enough talking already?* And oh I need the bathroom now but it's already coming out as I say *I'm never going to fall in love with you, Eddie.*

10

Kay was fast asleep and Georgie was 'out with friends' — which for some years had been code for 'out doing God knows what' — when Will took a newly purchased notebook into his office. He cleared a space on the desk, opened the notebook at the first page and wrote the heading '1) Cynthia'. The fact that he had written the number '1' scared him, because this indicated that there were subsequent options; that if this did not work he would need to move on to numbers 2) and 3) and — God forbid — 4), or even 5). He was unwilling to consider failure. He would succeed. He would do everything in his power to get that woman's kidney. Okay, so the plan was not foolproof. He might not find her. She might be dead. If alive, she might not be compatible. He might not be, for that matter. No! Of course he would be. He had always been able to do everything for those girls. He would be able to do this too. From the moment he received the diagnoses, Will just *knew* that he would be compatible and refused to consider otherwise.

So both parents saving both children was

the best option — and should be attempted in full before any others were considered.

A week earlier, Will had spoken to the specialist about the test. 'Not yet,' he had said. The doctor, Mr Jamieson — who always had Van Morrison on repeat on the CD player in his office — nodded when Will told him there was no hurry. 'We can do that any time,' Will said. 'Just dotting the i's. Of course I'll be suitable.'

Sometimes a dreadful scenario crept into Will's thoughts, one where he has already been tested and is ready to donate, but there is no other donor available. In this situation, he would have a terrible, unthinkable decision to make. The thought of it made him slap his face with his hand (*Don't go there, Will. Don't even think about it. Not now. Not ever.*). Which option would this be above? Number 5, perhaps? He hit his forehead with his palm this time and said 'No!' out loud. He would never choose. He would save Georgie and Kay — which meant having both donors in place at the same time — which meant finding Cynthia. She was their mother, after all. What mother would refuse? What mother would leave the fate of her beautiful children at the mercy of an unreadable, ever-increasing list — a list with at least 6,500 people on it — yet only 1,800 transplants had been carried out in the last twelve months?

He sighed, fear overtaking his attempt at confidence, because the sort of mother who might do the above is also the sort of mother who might bugger off to the shops and never come back.

The AA map route to Manchester Prison churned out of the printer. Was that all he needed for the journey tomorrow afternoon? He checked the list he'd written under the heading on the first page of his notebook.

1a) *Booking (Yes, he'd booked the prison visit.)*

1b) *ID (Yes, he had the necessary identification to get through the gate.)*

1c) *Cash (He had money, just in case — £200 to be exact, leaving his flex account with a grand total of £1790.56 until next payday, in two weeks' time.)*

Will took himself to the smallest bedroom upstairs and stared at the ceiling for several hours before falling asleep.

After Kay went off to school the following morning, he decided not to wake Georgie. The dialysis was really taking its toll on her. She needed her rest.

He was about to make himself breakfast when the doorbell rang.

'Hello, William,' his father said. 'We need to talk.'

His parents visited once a month for dinner, a routine which they had insisted on after Cynthia left. Each month Will dreaded it, Georgie tried to get out of it and Kay looked on the bright side. ('They're our grandparents, Georgie. They love us. You can't go out with friends!') Will believed these three hours gave his parents a 'get-out-of-guilt-free' card. They'd seen their son. Tick. Asked their granddaughters about school and netball and orchestra. Tick. So off they could tootle to their show-home house in North Queensferry, which was far enough away to make further contact (i.e. help) impossible. Will's father had been a major in the army. His mum a husband-follower who liked good port at dinner parties. They'd sent Will to boarding school aged nine, where he'd hidden his loneliness in books and music. After graduating they sent him off to uni in St Andrews, where — much to their disapproval — he buried himself in films and filmy types. As a result, Will didn't know his parents at all. Thus far, he had no regrets. What he knew of them, he didn't like. Will's father had retired following the death of his uber-wealthy parents, leaving him enough money to buy twenty-three flats in Spain. He decided to rent them out and asked Will if he would like to manage the rentals for him. ('It's all very well wasting time on some Mickey Mouse media course, but it's the real world now, William. You're a father! You need to support your family.') The job involved advertising the properties, banking money and talking to people about the firmness of the beds, proximity to beach and pool facilities and the likelihood of rain. For years, Will had logged onto the computer each day with a loud sigh. It was possibly the loneliest and most tedious job in the world. Sometimes he prayed that a film idea would pop into his brain like it used to when he was at St Andrews. It never did.

'Rentals were down 30 per cent this year,' Will's father said. He was in one of his golfing ensembles — well-ironed grey trousers, black and red and grey argyle V-neck jumper. He'd obviously planned the visit to coincide with a round at Loch Lomond. As if Will cared about the rentals at the moment. As if it bothered him that Brits were staying home for their holidays this year.

'Thing is, we can't afford to keep them. Bad time to sell, bottom's out of the market, over-supply and what not, but I'm afraid we have no option.'

As Will made him a cup of coffee he wondered if he should throw it over his father's head. He hadn't seen him since *that* phone call, and he wanted to talk about the credit crunch!

That phone call was the first Will had made after Kay's diagnosis. He didn't beat around the bush. He asked his mother outright. 'Would one or both of you be willing to be tested?'

After a pause that was long enough to answer his question, Will's mother said they'd have to talk it over.

Will's father emailed two days later. 'William, we are still thinking about it. Obviously there might be issues because of our age. Have you put the new photographs of the pool on holidaylettings.com?'

'Here you go,' Will said, recalling the email angrily and placing the mug of Nescafé on the bench. He was throwing it over his father's head in his head. He hadn't written this option in his notebook yet, but as he sipped his coffee he decided it would be option no. 2).

They both drank it as fast as they could while Will answered questions that did not involve being an unemployed single parent with children who might die.

When he left, Will grabbed his keys and found himself walking around to Linda's house.

★ ★ ★

'You're crying,' Will said when she finally answered the door.

'It's the tears give it away,' she said, shutting it behind him.

Over a bottle of Highland Spring mineral water, they took turns to unload. They both had good reasons to. Linda's involved a mobile phone that rang at 2155 the previous night. At first, she ignored it, thinking it was the radio or a car alarm. But when it rang again at 2157, she followed the twinkle tone upstairs, into the bedroom, and into the fitted wardrobes she'd paid a handsome joiner a fortune to build, and into a pair of trousers.

Her husband, the silly moo, had left his phone in his jeans before heading off on business again.

The phone stopped ringing by the time she found it. She wasn't the kind to pry into her husband's business — partly because she wasn't very interested in him any more and partly because he was bald and fat now and

66

she felt confident that no one would want him.

WHAT TIME DO YOU ARRIVE? a text from the same number that had just called read.

I'VE BEEN WAITING AN HOUR, said the next.

WHERE R U?

I'M WEARING THE PANTIES YOU BOUGHT ME . . .

*   *   *

It was pretty clichéd, Will supposed, to wipe tears from a crying woman's cheek then move in for a kiss. Like snogging someone shitfaced at a club. A bad way to start. An accident. But that's how Will and Linda ended up in bed, with a tear wipe, a kiss and the following request:

'Do you mind if I hit you?'

Will thought for a moment and then said 'I'd actually rather you didn't.'

'You deserve to be hit, fucking a married woman.'

He turned to face her in bed. So this was the real Linda: scary while naked. He preferred the fully clad version. 'Do I?'

'You do. You've been a very bad boy. If my husband finds out he'll hit you even harder, might even kill you.'

'Can't I just feel a bit guilty? Go to confession or something?'

'This is your confession. What have you done, Good Guy?'

'I've fucked a married woman, but her husband is cheating . . . '

'What did you say?'

'Her husband is cheating on her.'

'No, the first bit. Say it again.'

'I fucked a married woman. Please don't hit me too hard.'

Linda did not comply with this instruction. She grabbed a wooden spoon from the bedside table and walloped Will full throttle on the balls. Will cried. He wished he'd noticed the wooden spoon earlier.

'I'm going to go home now,' he said, wiping his eyes, holding his testicles and struggling into his clothes.

'Ah, that was fantastic,' she said as Will finally managed his shoes. 'I needed that. Call me later, yeah?'

'Sure. When I get back from Manchester.'

11

'Your daughter was supposed to visit me,' Heath said from his side of the crescent-shaped chair.

Heath had put on weight since Will last saw him. The anger in his jaw was puffy. He oozed a stench of airless sweat, socks and spunk. Fat, stinky and incarcerated, he still scared the living daylights out of Will, who held one hand in the other to try and contain the trembling. They'd never spoken without Cynthia present and Will realised an uncomfortable lynch-pin was better than none at all. These were her men, her two men, sitting opposite each other, eyeing each other: one with begging terror, the other with violent disdain.

'She's not well,' Will said. Did he stammer? He hoped not. Did it matter if Heath knew how frightened he was? Did it matter that Will seemed infantile, tiny and feeble in comparison to this brute? Perhaps not, but it annoyed Will no end that Heath Jones still held all the power despite his prison-issue polo shirt.

'So?'

'It's both the girls, Cynthia's girls.' (How long since he'd said her name out loud? The hot sound of it travelled through his veins.)

'Like I said, *So?*'

'So I want to find my wife.'

'Wife!' Heath paused for a dramatic gangster-style laugh then spoke with a snigger. 'Do you still take hours to cum? She hated that.'

'Where is she?' Will's hands had separated and were now visibly shaking as they rested on top of his notebook and pen.

He was red. He knew he was red. Inside the red was Cynthia's voice saying, 'Get off me, will you? Can you not tell I've finished?'

'What's it worth to you?' Heath moved closer. His breath smelt of pus.

Will suggested one hundred pounds.

'Actually, no thanks, mate,' Heath said, sliding down his chair, getting comfortable. 'I'm more than happy to do an old friend a favour.'

Will hesitated. Heath's fixed smile unnerved him. 'Well, thank you,' he managed, after a long pause.

'No problems.' Heath leant forward, scribbled something on Will's notebook, and stood up.

Oh no, Will thought, he wants to shake

hands. Is there any way I can get out of shaking hands?

There wasn't. Will tried very hard to remain expressionless as Heath sealed the deal. This was not possible. It hurt, a lot, and Will's eyes narrowed with pain before filling with liquid.

Heath turned to leave. He was almost out the door when he stopped and said, 'Tell me when you've found her, eh?'

As Heath disappeared into the bosom of the prison, Will inhaled deeply. He wasn't sure, but he wondered if he'd forsaken breathing for several minutes beforehand.

Half an hour later, Will left Strangeways having achieved two things:

He had Cynthia's last known address — a year ago, she had lived in a flat in Finsbury Park, London.

And he owed Heath Jones a favour.

★　★　★

It was dark by the time Will found the street. He had to park two hundred metres from the address, which was a large Victorian terraced house near the tube station. At the front door, he knocked three times and waited.

The door had once contained a rectangle of glass. This had been boarded over with unpainted MDF. The doormat was frayed and filthy. Will stared at it, trying to remain calm. Would he see her any second? Would she be as enthralling as she was back then? How would it make him feel? Suddenly, a piece of paper appeared on top of the mat. Someone inside had posted a note underneath the door. He picked it up.

'Put the money through the bay window at the front,' the note said.

What? Will read it again, knocked again. Nothing happened. He walked out into the front garden (a strip of concrete, really, three feet long). One of the windows in the bay was open about two inches.

'I don't have money,' he said through the crack. The bent metal venetians prevented him from seeing inside.

'Well fuck off, then,' a woman's voice said. 'No money, no gear.'

'I don't want gear. My name is Will Marion. Cynthia, is that you?'

The pause that followed was interminable. Was it her? Was she fixing her hair for him? Or jumping out the back window, running through lanes, hailing a taxi?

He moved back to the front door and waited. Oh God, oh God, the door was opening.

'You know Cynthia?' The woman before

him was about twenty-three. Seven stone at the most. Track marks. Her eyes two empty ponds.

'I'm her ex-husband. Can I see her?'

'Dunno.'

'Is she there?'

'Maybe.'

He would have to pay, he realised.

'Go get her,' he said, placing a neat ten-pound note in her hand.

She put the money in her pocket. 'She's not here. She left a year ago. Fucking slag. Stole our gear. Far as I know, she went to India with her friend. You find her, tell her we've not forgotten.'

'Where in India?'

The woman had no idea.

'What friend?'

'That's all I know,' she said, scratching her arm so hard it made Will's arm feel sore.

★ ★ ★

Before heading home, Will visited someone he should have visited thirteen years earlier.

Meredith was a foster carer, the last person, in fact, to attempt to parent Cynthia, who had arrived at her house at the age of fifteen. Cynthia loved her, said Meredith was the only adult who ever really understood her as a child. Will hadn't seen Meredith and her then-husband, Brett, since they'd driven all the way to Glasgow for the wedding. The wedding! Cynthia had said she wanted something unconventional and humanist. Somehow, she ended up deciding on the University Chapel and an old hotel in Dumbartonshire. It couldn't have been more conservative. She even wore white and asked Meredith's husband to give her away.

'Brett died a year ago,' Meredith said sadly. 'An infected finger ended up poisoning his blood and destroying his insides.'

Since the wedding, Meredith had changed from a middle-aged cuddly person into a fat old person. Will counted four chins as she retrieved a postcard from her magnet-infested fridge.

'Merry,' it read. 'You HAVE to come here. There are so many colours!'

The picture on the front of the postcard showed a gorgeous beach with cafes selling lassi. 'Chapora, Goa', it read. It was dated eleven months ago.

* * *

An accident near Penrith and road works at Dumfries meant it took Will eight hours to drive home. The house was quiet — he

74

assumed both girls were in bed asleep.

So her last known address was in India. He went to his office, took out his notebook and wrote: 'India — Go there and try to find her myself?'

As he jotted pros and cons neatly, he realised this was not a viable option. He couldn't leave the girls to cope with dialysis alone.

Next, he googled her name — using her maiden name, Burns, her married name, Marion, and Heath's surname, Jones. Pages and pages later, he realised the search was too wide, and that it was unlikely she'd have built an internet presence considering her busy drug-taking and itinerant lifestyle.

He searched Facebook. The Cynthias with the right surnames as well as head shots bore no resemblance. He began messaging the ones without photos, but became disheartened when he realised he would need to send thousands of them.

He tried Twitter. Got nowhere.

Looked up online missing person's databases. Needed a drink.

Phoned the UK embassy in Delhi. It rang out for hours, and when someone finally answered the phone they dismissed him with a muffled reply about 'not being in' and hung up.

Knowing he needed help with this, he googled Glasgow private detectives. In the end, an agency called The Hunters and Collectors leapt out. Will emailed them the basic details, having decided that he would give the agency three weeks to find her. Failing that, he might have to write another heading on the third page of his notebook.

12

The thing I noticed most about being sick was getting annoyed at absolutely everything. Don't get me wrong, I've always been a grumpy arse, but once I started dialysis, grumpiness became an inadequate description of my reaction to the hot water being off (*What lice-infected fuckwit moron used all the water?*), to my keys going missing (*When I find the bastard who hid my keys I'm going to kill them!*), to my favourite white T-shirt coming out of the washing grey and splotchy (*Dad, you put black stuff in with the washing. What's wrong with you — early onset Alzheimer's? Next-door's cat could run a house better!*).

I got home from nose-dick Eddie's at around two in the morning. I must have fainted or fallen asleep and he was kind enough not to kick me out. Gathering my clothes, I left a note on the cardboard-box bedside table: 'Sorry for talking shite and puking on your bed,' then hailed a taxi on Pollokshaws Road.

Dad and Kay were asleep in bed and I was still sick as a dog. I had a quick shower then fell into bed.

When I woke up the following evening — day and night had switched places since I dropped out of school to be a dead person — I realised that Dad wasn't there. He had actually gone to find my mother, like he said. There was a note on the hall table: 'In Manchester, back tonight. There's soup in the fridge.' I ate some cereal and tried to imagine him on a mission. Ha! Dad on a mission. How would he get information out of a murderer in Strangeways? How would he get my mother's kidney? He couldn't even get me to set the table.

There was nothing I could do to distract myself. Had he found her? Would he come home with news of her? The television was on, but I was staring beyond the screen for hours, excited, nauseous, terrified.

Kay had the biggest bedroom — the bay-windowed one upstairs overlooking the front garden. I'd always wanted this room, but what would be the point of asking? Kay always got the best things — while I got the murky brown teddy, she got the blue one; I got the tiny white radio alarm clock thing, she got the full CD player with speakers; I wasn't allowed to go on a date till I was fifteen, she went to the movies with the orchestra guy at fourteen. But hell, even I had to admit she deserved to get better stuff than me.

I sat on her bed. 'Do you think he'll find her?'

'Dunno,' she said.

'What do you reckon she'll say?'

'Don't care.' Kay hadn't even bothered to look up from her chemistry book.

Fucking Kay. How could she not care? 'Well, when he finds her, I'm getting *her* kidney. You can have his shitey one,' I said, slamming her door shut.

★ ★ ★

I was asleep on the sofa when Dad woke me the following afternoon. 'Georgie, Georgie,' he said. I opened my eyes excitedly, only to be smacked down with the following: 'I didn't find her. She went to India a year ago.'

I closed my eyes. What was the point of having hope nowadays? Nothing good ever happened.

'So that's it?' I said, eyes still closed.

'I'm hiring a private detective.'

'Whereabouts in India?' I asked.

He showed me a postcard she'd sent her foster mum. Why had she never sent me one? I touched her words. She'd also touched this card, my mum. I turned it over. The beach looked beautiful. I wouldn't have gotten in her way. I would have been happy sitting at

79

that cafe watching her be happy.

'All we can do is wait,' Dad said.

'Excellent. I'm good at that.'

★ ★ ★

That night at dialysis, someone had disappeared and someone had arrived.

The rumours about forty-year-old Jimmy being next to go were right. His transplant was a belter. No problems at all, so far. Lucky guy.

The new boy was Brian and he totally looked like a Brian. He had glasses and neat hair and square shoulders. He and his Alfred seemed very at ease with each other.

'How old are you?' he asked, and I told him seventeen.

'I'm sixteen,' he said. I wished I hadn't added a year.

'Do you think I'm yellow?' I asked.

'No,' he said. 'Am I?'

'No,' I lied again.

When we'd both been purified, I asked Brian if he wanted to go for a drink. Since the whole Eddie endeavour, I knew I couldn't fall in love sober.

'Why don't you come to mine?' he said. 'The olds are away and I've got some skunk.'

It was looking like a match made in heaven.

'Are you scared?' he asked me, sitting cross-legged on the floor of his teenage bedroom.

'I've decided not to think about it.'

'How can you not?' He took a grey ring binder from his tidy desk and opened it. Inside were 500 sheets of lined A4 paper. On each line was a date — the first was three years ago. Each day, the sad fuck had marked a cross against the date.

'Each time the list gets longer, I add the days at the end. According to my current status, I have 1,350 days to wait for a kidney. That's 771 times at dialysis.'

He'd highlighted four dates each week to indicate his stints at the unit.

'Jesus Christ, does this not drive you bonkers?'

'Does it not drive you?'

'I think about more important things,' I said.

'Like?'

'Like falling in love.'

He leant in as if to say: *I am the one you will fall in love with. I am here to fill that role. With me, you will never be scared.*

But Brian fainted before reaching me. Both of us should've known to go home to bed after dialysing. Twice in a row I'd broken this cardinal rule.

81

If Brian hadn't peed himself at the point of unconsciousness, we might have remained friends. Unfortunately, some of the pee ruined some of his A4 pages. He'd probably do new ones as soon as possible, the retard.

★ ★ ★

Despite a distinct lack of success thus far, I still felt it better to concentrate on finding love than on the facts of my life, which were few and negative. I had dropped out of school and was therefore qualificationless. And I was indeed yellow. My next love-falling attempt told me so when I asked.

'You are,' said Reece, 'but I like yellow girls.'

Reece was a nurse. He was around twenty, cuddly (one stone overweight) and funny. He'd been on duty six times in a row since Brian peed on his home-made waiting list.

'Is it appropriate to fall in love with a patient?' I asked Reece one session. (Brian heard, but he didn't look. He hadn't looked at me since the whole pant-pissing incident two weeks earlier.) Reece had brought me DVDs three times in a row, each more datey than the last. He definitely wanted me.

'Totally inappropriate,' he said.

Pause.

Lean in.

Whisper.

'But I like inappropriate girls.'

Reece met me at a pub called the Bothy. A crappy band was playing on the quarter-inch stage. Grungy types stood and swayed (not too much) at the alternative sounds.

It's probably not a great idea to take class-A drugs when you've just come out of dialysis. Up there with bananas. But, hell, I was with a nurse — and he thought it'd be okay. So in the bathroom, I snorted some of his powder through a cut-to-size straw. Sometimes dancing comes naturally. Sometimes not. When I got back onto the dance floor, my arms seemed ridiculously large and no matter how hard I tried to feel the music, all I could feel was *them*, dragging my shoulders down as if they were ropes with bricks on the end.

To add to that, a guy with sunglasses on was standing at the bar staring at me. He was much cuter than Reece, and I wanted to impress him. I wanted Reece to bugger off so I could make a move on him. He smiled at me, the sunglasses guy. And romantic-comedy style, I responded by immediately walking into a pillar some fucker had put right in the middle of the room. Somehow I managed to stay standing.

'You okay?' Reece asked. His face was bright red. His eyes tiny pricks of black. He didn't really want to know if I was okay. He was a bastard.

'I'm going home,' I said, trying not to think about the gorgeous guy at the bar and the enormity of my arms. (What if I couldn't hold them up any more? What would happen? Would they drop off?)

'Let me take you,' Reece said, putting his hand on my back. His hand was as red as his face. Reece was a big red blob.

'I'm never going to fall in love with you, Reece,' I said, staggering out, my arms a few steps behind me.

13

Will had dealt with Georgie's mood swings for years. Well, not so much swings as heart-wrenching unhappiness which manifested itself either in tearful hopelessness (*What if I die tomorrow? If I'm run over by a bus tomorrow I will have lived a shit life!*) or in terrifying fits of rage. (Once, she threw a mug of tea at the patio doors because the post was late. Will can't remember now what letter she'd been expecting.) How on earth, he had wondered, would she cope if anything serious happened? When, aged seven, a friend decided not to come to her birthday party because 'she just didn't feel like going to a party', Georgie vowed never to talk to the offender again, and never did. When an imminent maths test (second year) caused her to yell out of her window to the forty terraces in the street (*My father is a fuckwit and maths is a fucking waste of time*). When, on a family walk at the nearby wind farm, her new jeans sodden from the rain, she fell to the ground and screamed 'I hate living here. I am not stepping foot outside again until you say we can move to Spain!'

So how on earth would this melodramatic knot of anger react to a life-threatening illness?

It surprised Will, because Georgie's behaviour changed only marginally. Her rage just turned up a notch to unbridled rage.

It was after midnight when Georgie finally arrived home from the Bothy, which — unbeknownst to her — was the very place her parents had met all those years ago.

'You look terrible,' Will said.

'Fuck you,' she replied.

'What did you say?'

'Thank you,' she lied.

Will decided, as usual, to let her get away with it. What was the point? And anyway, he had too many other things to worry about. There was mail to not open, bills to not pay. It'd been two weeks since his father had taken away his only income. Since then, he'd watched the reminder notices pile up at the door. The bank had started phoning already, so he'd turned all phones to silent, head firmly in the sand.

'So are you sleeping with Linda Stewart?' Georgie said. She was holding his mobile phone.

'No.' He wasn't lying. They'd had an icky scary screw a fortnight earlier, but her husband had come home the following day

86

and he'd heard nothing since. Technically, they'd slept together but they weren't *sleeping together*.

'She's left a message on your phone,' Georgie said, pressing LOUDSPEAKER on the mobile.

'Give me that. It's mine,' he said, but Linda's voice was already in the room. 'Will, can I come over after the girls are asleep? He's still here. But it's over. I need to see you.'

'Blah . . . how disgusting,' Georgie said. 'I have images. Youch.'

'Please don't listen to my messages.' Georgie completely ignored her father, taking the phone off loudspeaker, and pressing 3 to listen to the next.

'Mr Marion, I'm calling from the Hunters and Collectors,' a male voice said into Georgie's ear. 'I have some news . . . '

14

The day before Preston MacMillan of the Hunters and Collectors Private Detective Agency had phoned Will Marion with the good news, Cynthia had been lying on the beach at Dahab, in Egypt. 'It was the more difficult option,' she was saying. 'Leaving was actually the brave thing to do.'

'Bloody right. You're brave's what you are. You're a brave woman.' She couldn't for the life of her recall the name of the man she was talking to. He handed back the photograph Cynthia had swapped for his bong. In the photograph were two beautiful little girls, aged three.

It was his turn with the bong.

'A selfish person would have stayed,' Cynthia said, touching the photograph.

'Yep.' The man exhaled thick smoke into the blue sky. 'You're not fuckin' selfish. I can see a mile away you're a woman with guts.'

It was Cynthia's turn again. She tucked her photo into her money belt, took the bong and inhaled. Smoky pride filled her up. What a woman. What a girl. Someone less gutsy would've stayed with a man she didn't love, would have hung around and been a bad mother, ruining those two children for life, as she and Heath had been ruined by their respective screw-ups for mothers.

'What's your name again?' she asked the man.

'Peter,' he said. 'But my friends call me Peter.'

They laughed till they were rolling on the carpet that had been set out for them on the sand, a carpet they were supposed to be thinking about purchasing. 'Can we lie on it for a bit?' the bloke called Peter had asked the carpet salesman two hours earlier. He and Cynthia had met in the carpet shop, and immediately recognised kindred spirits in each other's long straggly hair, bright eastern clothing and general fucked-out-of-their-mindedness. 'We don't want to buy nothing too scratchy,' the man called Peter had said.

The salesman, probably the most patient man in the universe, did as they had asked, laying the carpet on the sand before his beach-front shop, and then watched over them as they smoked on top of it. (His best carpet!)

'I'm Cynthia . . . ' she said to Peter, holding her sore stomach, 'but my friends call me . . . ' It was no use, she couldn't say it. It was too funny.

'That's it!' the Egyptian salesman said. 'Get off my rug!'

He pulled it from underneath them, leaving Cynthia and Peter guffawing on the beach.

Over the last year, Cynthia had probably slept with around one hundred men. She was proud of this fact, considering that she was over thirty, okay, over forty, all right all right, the next one, then, but only just. She looked good with clothes on — slim and tanned — and men rarely changed their minds once they saw the stretch marks, track marks, pancake tits and cellulite underneath her youthful vibrant clothing. She'd lost count exactly, but Peter was probably about number 101 and she gave him the attention he deserved in the tent afterwards, asking for little in return.

She had never been selfish. She was an artist, yes, could've been a very important one if she'd been the type to lick arse, but she was not selfish. Hence, she left Will Marion all those years ago for *his* sake. Will, as uninspired and ordinary as he was, would be a good parent. He would bring the girls up to be good people. She needed to leave so he could do that.

'Can I sing you a song?' she asked the Peter guy a few hours later. He was asleep. She shook his shoulder. 'Do you want to hear me sing? Peter! Peter!'

'What?' He would rather have stayed asleep.

'I'm a singer. You get a song for free.'

'Excellent,' he said, shutting his eyes.

Something had happened to her voice in the years since she'd left Scotland. It almost hurt to sing, and she feared it might have hurt even more to listen. She sang, nevertheless, and Peter had the courtesy to clap (eyes still closed) once she'd finished.

She lay back down beside number 101 (ish) and stared at the roof of yet another tent. She missed Heath the same way she missed heroin. She knew he was bad for her, that he hurt her, that he hurt lots of people, that sometimes, when he was angry, he'd scare her so much she'd lock herself in the bathroom for hours on end. How long till his release now? Would she ever stop loving him? Could she ever stop wanting him?

She'd never been in love with Will Marion. She liked to try things and at the time she felt she ought to try contentment. In the end, though, suburban family life, a mediocre man and two demanding children could never be more than an interesting experiment.

Heath, on the other hand — where was that photograph? Was it in her money belt? Oh God, she didn't lose it on the beach, did she? She needed a smoke, she found a smoke, lit it, and emptied the belt of its money, passport and snapshots until the small photograph of Heath took the panic away — oh Heath, he had always been much more than an experiment.

They'd both been fourteen years old when they met at the house in Stoke Newington. He'd been with the foster family for several months — what were their names again? John and Petra? Jane and Peter? — she couldn't recall because she'd only stayed for a few days.

'Cynthia, this is Heath. He's the same age as you!' Peter or John had said. Heath was already six feet tall. And very good looking. And he had fags.

'Give us one,' Cynthia said when her new foster father disappeared into the kitchen.

'Five new pence,' he said.

'A shillin'? Give us a fag, I'll give you a dance.'

'Why would I want to see you dance?'

'Because I'll do it naked.'

Obviously it was a deal. In the garden shed, Cynthia writhed like a post-pubescent — excited to show off the breasts and hair that had recently sprouted. Her dance moves had been perfected in her previous foster home. The social workers' vigilant vetting had ensured that no black or mixed-race children were cared for by the white carers, that there was adequate square footage in the house to accommodate orphans of both genders, but it had not delved as far as the magazine drawer in the family room, which housed a fantastic variety of porn.

Heath was in love. He gave Cynthia the first of many cigarettes and so began a beautiful romance. In Heath's attic bedroom at 2 a.m. that night they took their first acid tab together. At 4 p.m. in Boots the Chemists the following day they stole two packets of condoms and three packets of throat lozenges — they had no intention of using the latter. The day after that they stayed off school together. That night after not going to school they wrote a song, smoked grass, kissed, danced, laughed, touched, screwed . . .

Oh boy, did they screw. Angrily.

The day after, they ran away.

After that, they were in love and insepa-rable.

One last year with foster carers — the lovely Meredith, who surprised them by not being afraid of them, even appearing to like them.

After that they formed a band and lived life to the full. They did experiments, dared each other to break boundaries (Take this drug!

Sing that song! Break into that shop! Seduce that girl while I watch!).

It was passion, Cynthia supposed. Was it passion to want someone so much that you're willing to put up with the odd beating? To work for him, sometimes, if there was no money for gear, him keeping watch in the living room while she made money in the bedroom? To worry sometimes, that he might go further than a small fracture, that he might go so far as to kill her?

He spent a total of ninety-five days out of prison between the ages of twenty-five and thirty-three. His offences were mainly serious assaults and drugs charges but his sentences were always extended because of his behaviour inside — rioting, drug use, hostage taking, assaults and one dirty protest.

During these years, Cynthia visited regularly, but when she turned thirty-three she decided to try and go straight. Or was Cynthia becoming an everyday woman with an everyday biological clock?

'I've met someone,' she told Heath in the visits room of Saughton Prison one rainy November.

'I dare you to marry him,' Heath snarled.

So she did, but not because of what Heath said, which was really a warning, but because Will, she thought, might be the answer to her

94

problems. He might wean her off heroin and, more importantly, off Heath.

She was too scared to visit Heath again.

At first, Cynthia quite enjoyed being mollycoddled. But Will Marion was a bore and sobriety was over-rated. She was glad when Heath appeared on her doorstep and said: 'Well, if it isn't Mrs Marion.' With Heath to make love to on the sly, she thought, perhaps she could handle the drudgery of suburban life. Perhaps she could handle being a mother.

★ ★ ★

As Cynthia lay in the tent in Dahab, Peter snoring beside her, she congratulated herself once more for leaving Will all those years ago. She had made the right decision. She was not cut out for that life, and she would only have made it impossible for Will and the girls. She drew the last of her cigarette and lay back to imagine Heath. The years after she left Will blurred in a drugs haze — how many flats did she and Heath squat in? Who were they living with? She couldn't recall. But it was fun, wasn't it? Scary sometimes, like the time Heath stole a car for them to get home from a club and closed his eyes as they approached a red light. 'If we're meant to be together the universe will protect us,' he said. 'Ten seconds? Fifteen?' He ignored Cynthia's screams and pushed her arms away from the wheel with his elbows. 'If God loves us, we'll survive. If not, I don't want to live. One, two, three . . . ' Turned out, God loved Heath and Cynthia a whole bunch more than Miriam from Jedburgh and the Ford Escort she'd just bought. Then there was the time a punter did something she didn't like and she protested and yelled and Heath came into the bedroom and beat the man's head against the window pane until he stopped moving. But being scared was similar to fun, wasn't it?

He got life at the age of forty-two — which meant ten years minimum in HM Prison Manchester. Cynthia waited, and waited. She tried rehab. She tried singing again. She tried making new friends at the local supermarket. She tried to make the days pass until he was out. But that last rejection was too much. She decided to deal with his absence the way she had when coke supplies dwindled in Glasgow in 1991. She accepted it.

She moved on to something else. She withdrew. She got off the heavy stuff — indeed she stole what was left from the dealers she was living with in Finsbury Park, sold it, and got on a plane.

Zzzz . . . Someone was fiddling with the zipper of the tent. 'Excuse me?' a man said from outside. 'Is there a Cynthia Marion in there?'

15

It had been two weeks since the weed visited Heath in prison. Since then, Heath had felt jubilant and powerful. As he lay in his bunk listening to the night noises of the hall, he smiled. He'd come in handy all right, the poofter. That's what he and Cynth used to call him (although sometimes she became a bit defensive — 'He's not gay, Heath! Don't be so judgemental!'). If he wasn't gay, then what was he? He was pathetically small. Around five-nine, five-ten at the most. And what were those shoulders all about? They'd work for a girl, maybe, but not a grown man. Jesus, why did she ever bother with the guy, dare or no dare?

'Well, if it isn't Mrs Marion!' Heath had said when he arrived on her doorstep. She looked about as freshly married as a widow of eighty-five. 'May I come in?'

And so Cynthia let him in. Let him take her in his car and in his flat. Told him all about her twice-a-week sex life with Will Marion.

'He tells me he loves me constantly!' she told Heath, and he laughed. 'He tells me I have a beautiful flat stomach! He goes on and on, for an hour sometimes.'

Sounded to Heath like better sex could be had in the prison showers than in their marital bedroom. The guy seemed like a pathetically grateful teenager, without the physique to match.

God knows how the three years happened. Cynthia went on some nutcase mission to be normal — bonking Heath non-stop in the meantime, of course — and he sat by and waited till she was finished, distracting himself with a few bimbos along the way.

And now he was back. The little poofter. Back for more.

Oh, he'd get more all right.

★　★　★

Heath pointed his torch at the photograph of Cynthia that he'd pinned to the underside of the top bunk. He knew why Cynthia had left eleven months earlier. He'd promised her he'd get out back then and he was sure he would — if it wasn't for that fucking yap-yap social worker, the greasy little prick. He understood that she didn't want the days to drag like they did for him. But he never doubted she'd be there for him when he got out. She knew better than to cross him like that.

16

Preston MacMillan wasn't calling Will's mobile from his office. There were two good reasons for this. Firstly, he was in Egypt. And secondly, he didn't have an office. The Hunters and Collectors Private Detective Agency was actually the cupboard off the living room of his West End tenement flat. For his birthday, Preston's mum had paid Fred, her seventy-year-old neighbour, to decorate the cupboard in preparation for his advanced higher exams. Under her not-very-close supervision, Fred put shelves all the way to the ceiling at one end, a brand-spanking-new Ikea desk at the other and a big swivelly chair betwixt. 'Thanks, Mum!' Preston had said. 'This is really amazing.'

'Nothing is too good for my boy, you know that, don't you, Preston? You know I love you?' his mother replied. 'Now come and blow out the candles.'

Preston was seventeen years old.

★ ★ ★

The detective agency idea had come to Preston one Sunday afternoon two years earlier. He was watching *Dexter*, an American television show featuring a serial killer. The thing about this killer was that he turned his problem into something positive by only murdering really badass people. *Ka-ching!* Preston sat up straight. It was perfect. He liked to follow people, women mainly. And he'd been in trouble for it once — oh, but Briony was worth the referral to the Children's Panel he got for standing over her bed that time. But he also followed males — James Marshall, for instance, who had a better train set than him aged seven. He'd followed him since the train set: as he rode his bike to the secret hideout aged nine, as he played rugby down Giffnock aged eleven, as he kissed Rebecca Gordon behind the scout hall aged fourteen, as he set fire to wheelie bins aged sixteen. He always kept mementos, too. In an old computer box on the top shelf of his new office, a growing collection reminded him of his subjects. James Marshall's water bottle. Susie Davidson's locker key. Maria McDowall's glove. Pauline Bryce's nail polish remover.

The idea was genius — why not follow people who needed to be followed?

101

The name — The Hunters and Collectors — came to him one night when he was rifling through his mother's bedroom cupboard (not for any reason, just because he liked to rifle). In a small shoe box, his mother also kept keepsakes, but only of her electrocuted husband. One was a CD of an Australian band, The Hunters and Collectors. Preston didn't even listen to it, but the name was perfect.

The agency brought together all the skills he'd honed over his teenage years — he was a capable and thorough researcher, an able computer hacker, excellent at sifting through people's rubbish, genius at hiding behind trees, shrubs or fences while looking through windows with or without binoculars, and he was accomplished at breaking into houses. Mostly, though, he was dedicated. Once he set his sights on someone, he did not give up.

So far, he had successfully found a missing teenager and brought her home to her worried-to-the-point-of-pissed-out-of-her-mind mother (he kept one of her fake eyelashes); he had captured photographic evidence of a gay love affair for a distraught wife (kept a used condom); and exonerated a man who was not having an affair but watching his choice of televisual entertainment in a rented flat as far away as possible from his nagging partner (the remote control).

The first message from William Marion read thus:

Hello, I wonder if you can help me. My estranged wife, Cynthia Marion, left for India a little over one year ago. Her address before this was Flat 1a, Digby Crescent, Finsbury Park, London. I urgently need to find her. Our two teenage daughters are ill and both need kidney transplants. Can you please contact me via email or on my mobile.

Kind regards,

Will Marion.

In his cupboard office, where he was supposed to be revising chemistry (Did his mother not realise he had learnt it all months earlier? That he would blitz his exams without so much as revising a single page?), Preston emailed back immediately.

I am happy to help. I am highly skilled in this area, and have a 100% success rate in tracing missing persons. Due to the highly delicate and confidential nature of my assignments, I prefer to communicate via email and ask that you delete all messages from your hard drive once the information has been passed on. My fee is £500 per week plus travel expenses (you say she may be in India, which means I will probably need to travel there and will require an emergency contingency fund to cover the costs involved). One week's fee is a non-refundable deposit. This should be paid into my PayPal account using this email address. If you would like me to take the case, please do this immediately and provide me with the following details:

— your full name and address

— your estranged wife's full name, any aliases, her date of birth, old and recent photographs, bank account details, friends, boyfriends, offending history, psychiatric or medical history, and any other information you feel may be helpful. The more information I have, the easier it will be for me to find her.

Once I have received the initial payment and these details, I will get to work without delay.

Yours,

The Hunters and Collectors

Will got back to him at once, depositing the first payment into his PayPal account and giving him all the information he could think of, including Heath's details, Janet's address, Meredith's address, a brief summary of what he knew about Cynthia's addiction issues, and the name of her band.

Just as Preston had promised, he set to work straight away.

17

Zzzzz. Cynthia unzipped the tent. The sound didn't wake the Peter man she'd shagged and sang at.

'Who's asking?' she said, squinting at the teenager before her. The sun stabbed her hung-over eyes. As they adjusted, she noticed that he looked like a young James Dean. *How young is too young?* she wondered.

'Delivery boy,' Preston said. 'Can we get a coffee?'

'Depends what you're delivering.'

'News from a loved one,' he said. 'Meet you down the beach in ten.'

Cynthia immediately assumed the boy had come with news of Heath. Perhaps he'd gotten out — but that couldn't be right, he wasn't eligible for parole for another month at least. Unless he'd escaped. Heath had considered this before. The last time she visited him, in fact.

'I can't do this any more,' she'd said. 'If they reject you again, I can't sit around and wait.'

He got that look in his eye he only got with Cynthia. A little-boy look, pleading.

106

'I'll wait for you, Heath, just not here. You understand?'

'I'll break out,' he said, grasping her hand, begging her not to leave him.

'Heath, promise me you won't do that. You've got another year at most — you'll get parole next time! Don't try anything daft or you'll get another ten years and my tits'll be doubling for my slippers.'

Maybe he hadn't listened to her, Cynthia thought as she exited the tent. Maybe he'd packed himself into a large cardboard box and posted himself out the jail. Maybe he'd paid someone to fly a helicopter over the exercise yard and grabbed onto the feet of it, dangling his way to freedom. Cynthia's imagination was racing as she brushed her teeth and had a pee in the communal bathroom. She started running towards the beach, but was out of breath within seconds, so walked as fast as she could.

He was sitting, sunglasses on, at the first cafe in the strip. He'd undone two buttons to reveal several fine blond chest hairs. If he's over sixteen it's not illegal, Cynthia thought to herself, wetting her dry lips before sitting down beside him.

'I took the liberty of ordering for you,' the boy said. 'Sugar?'

'Cheers,' she said, adding three spoonfuls

to her cup of coffee and stirring.

'My name is Jonathan,' he lied. 'Your ex-husband asked me to find you.'

Cynthia choked on her first sip. It sprayed in Preston's face. He wiped it off with a serviette.

'What does he want?'

'Your kidney,' he said, which caused a second, far heavier, spraying.

* * *

The woman didn't look like Georgie at all, Preston thought. She had a touch of the substance-addled witch about her — frizzy unkempt hair, over-tanned undernourished skin, red cannabis eyes. No, Georgie was entirely different from her mother. Brown eyes, not blue, light brown hair not dark, and — even though she was seriously ill — Georgie looked a whole lot healthier than her mother. As Preston wiped recycled coffee from his face for the second time, he wondered what use this woman's organs would be anyway.

* * *

He'd started the search with the postcard from Goa. Once Will had deposited travel expenses into his account, he told his mum he was off to his friend's holiday house in the Highlands to cram for exams. She was an alcoholic and thick as two bricks, his mum. Preston often wondered how he wound up being so gifted. Maybe his dead dad had been a genius, but he doubted this — he'd electrocuted himself changing a light bulb, which didn't sound too clever to Preston. So maybe it was being somewhere on the autistic spectrum that made him a genius. He found this latter fact quite hilarious, imagined himself balancing, arms out, on a long wire beside loads of other window lickers, yelling at people in the real world below . . . 'Hey, you down there! Look at me! Here! Up here! On the spectrum!'

The flight to Mumbai gave him time to learn some Hindi and Urdu, which was helpful when it came to booking and finding the bus to Goa. He boarded it three hours after landing in Mumbai. In that time, Preston came to understand the saying, 'The British invented bureaucracy and the Indians perfected it.' He had to stand at four different counters to buy his bus ticket. Unlike several other white travellers, he didn't let the laboriousness of the process get him down. How would impatience help? With one hour to spare after buying his ticket, he asked a taxi driver to show him as much of the city as possible. Heavy traffic meant he saw only a very Westernised shopping street, including McDonald's — where he bought a chicken burger — and other taxis. He boarded the bus with five minutes to spare, placing himself on an aisle seat in the middle and putting a bag on the window seat so no one would sit next to him. Luckily, no one did. He would have hated it, especially if a Westerner had taken the seat. 'Where do you come from?' they would have asked before bombarding him with tales of their own lives, expecting eye contact and head nodding.

On the screen at the front of the bus, Bollywood videos played on a loop for the sixteen-hour journey. Bright people danced to loud screeching. Preston could imagine liking it for an hour or so, but sixteen was utter hell. A large sign was pinned onto the driver's cabin: 'Our introduction you. Cabin in the only for.' Preston spent a while trying to decipher the translation, and many hours looking out the window at the blackness of this strange night world, illuminated only by occasional advertisements: 'I drink Limca because I like it!' 'Help eradicate malaria!' and 'People with dignity eat Nepalese sausage!'

Somehow, Preston managed to fall asleep

and when he woke, tropical lushness had coloured the landscape. He disembarked in Mapusa. Perhaps if he'd been on holiday, he'd have taken more notice of this vibrant, happy city, its unpaved streets filled with colourful markets and roaming cows. But he was too excited about finding this woman, this Cynthia woman, who held the lives of her children somewhere underneath her skin.

The blue-striped bus to Chapora was cheap, but there was a good reason for this. It carried more passengers than three Scottish buses would. Passengers held on to the door for dear life as the sardines inside wriggled to shove them off. Preston was used to queuing, and had naively waited his turn to get on. By the time everyone else had managed to squash their way in, bar three locals with less vigorous elbows, the bus was impossible to enter and no amount of *Excuse me, but I have a ticket for this bus!* assisted his embarkation. As the bus was about to leave, one of the locals standing beside him walked around to the back and climbed a ladder onto the roof. The other two followed. 'Come on!' said the last. A minute later, Preston found himself sitting on the roof of a bus with a small railing around the side. It was liberating, Preston thought, to be on the roof of a bus. No one seemed to mind, and

— apart from having to duck for electrical cables and low bridges — it was wonderful to see the world from up there. Such a different world too, one where rows of men squatted together in fields and where women sold bright coloured powders in street stalls.

As soon as he arrived in the relaxed seaside village of Chapora, Preston began walking along the dirt-track of a main street, lined with small kiosks selling food and drink, asking shopkeepers and restaurant owners if they had seen Cynthia Marion, offering them several photographs to jog their memories. The fact that most people spoke English did not deter him from using his newfound linguistic skills.

'Ah, yes,' the thirty-third person he spoke to said. 'She stayed up in the red house off the beach track. Left a few weeks back. You can't miss it. It's bright red with a green roof.'

The owner of the red house, an Indian man in his fifties, recognised the image in the photograph immediately. 'She headed to Egypt,' he said. 'Ronny keeps in touch, I think.'

Ronny was on the loo out the back. Preston had been directed there so he walked down the side of the red house to find a small shed in the middle of the back yard. It was on stilts. Underneath it, three pigs, noses in the air, chomped noisily on something dark and hearty. Preston moved towards the pigs — they looked so cute eating hungrily at the foot of the shed. Suddenly, something appeared from a hole in the floor of the shed. The pigs pointed their noses up towards it, nibbling at the end before it had separated from wherever it came. When it fell to the ground, they gobbled greedily. A few moments later, a man aged around thirty-five exited the shed doing up his fly.

'Takes a while to get used to,' the man said, watching Preston watch the pigs eat the shit that he had just squeezed out. 'The little buggers have it in their gobs before it's out your arsehole. G'day, I'm Ronny.'

Preston didn't shake his hand. He followed him onto the veranda of the house, where Ronny had obviously taken up residence, and showed him the photograph of Cynthia.

'Yeah, Cynth. I was supposed to meet up with her, actually. Haven't quite gotten round to it. Party girl! Last time I saw her she was communicating with the moon on the beach in Anjuna.'

'How was she communicating with the moon?' Preston asked.

'There are ways here,' Ronny said. 'Usually involve tiny white tabs! One time, we got a lift back here after a party on an ice van. Most surreal journey of my life. Some guy with a really big face was sitting on the block of ice across from us. We couldn't stop laughing at how big it was. So bloody big! The van delivered ice to twenty-three beach cafes before we made it home. Our bums were numb.'

'How big was his face exactly?' Preston asked.

'I dunno. Probably not big at all. I'm going to a party tonight. I'll ask the moon for you.'

'I really don't think there'd be any point doing that,' Preston said.

'Right.' Ronny was staring at the young man in front of him. He was even weirder than the guy with the enormous face on the ice truck. 'She went to a place called Dahab in Egypt,' he said, hoping this news would be enough to make him go away immediately.

Unwilling to endure hours of Bollywood movies on the bus from Mapusa to Mumbai, Preston decided to pay a taxi driver to take him back to the airport. The haggling process went like this:

5,000 rupees. (Preston)
30,000 no less. (Taxi driver)
5,000 is my final offer. (Preston)
This price is (blows a raspberry). My taxi has a CD player. (Taxi driver)

5,000 is my final offer. (Preston)

I have to come all the way back again! This is good price for you! I will show you things tourists don't get to see. (Taxi driver)

5,000. I am not interested in things tourists don't get to see. (Preston)

My wife is dead and I have three children to support. (Taxi driver)

I am in a hurry. (Preston)

7,000, with music, and I show you two things tourists don't get to see. (Taxi driver)

6,000 and it's a deal. (Preston)

The drive was interminable, interrupted only by two lengthy stops at carpet shops which tourists don't get to see, apparently. The carpets were of such high quality and so cheap that Preston bought four with the money he'd saved from previous assignments. The carpets were to be posted to his home address the following week.

So easy, this job, Preston thought to himself, as he boarded his next plane. A piece of cake.

18

Cynthia had searched her soul many times in the past. Always successfully, she believed. And always, without exception, with the help of class-A drugs.

For over one year she had managed on a diet of cannabis and alcohol, bar the occasional hallucinogenic on the beaches of Southern India, but as soon as this young James Dean — who she would one day have, oh yes she would; Heath would like the story — as soon as this young thing told her that her children might die unless she sacrificed a piece of herself, the first thing that sprung to Cynthia's squidgy mind was heroin.

'What's in it for me?' she asked. Little did Preston know, Cynthia was already planning on returning home. Heath would be eligible for parole again any time and she had no intention of breaking her promise to him. She'd even started busking to save money for the ticket. So far, she had ten pounds.

'You'll save the life of one of your daughters.'

'Of course . . . ' This guy was an idiot.

'And . . . I assume you want to see your

boyfriend? I can pay for the ticket home.' He was becoming less of an idiot.

'Pay for the ticket and promise me something else,' she said.

'I can't promise till I know what it is.'

'I want two bags of heroin within an hour of reaching Glasgow.'

Preston picked the skin around his thumb. A neat line peeled off, which he placed in his tissue and folded. 'Make it two hours.'

'I'll pack my things,' Cynthia said, returning to her tent, imagining a syringe in every tall thin thing she spotted en route. Peter was still asleep inside the tent. His feet seemed pinprick pointy. She didn't wake him.

★ ★ ★

The unlikely pair retraced the last part of Preston's inbound journey, catching a bus to Cairo, where they booked a ticket to Glasgow via London.

Unfortunately, this meant waiting twelve hours in Cairo.

They used the time well.

Preston phoned his client in Glasgow. 'I have some good news,' he said into Will Marion's voicemail. 'I've found your wife.'

Cynthia phoned HMP Manchester. 'So he *is* still there?' she asked.

'Where else would he be?' came the predictably gruff officer.

She breathed a sigh of relief. He hadn't tried some dumb-arsed escape. 'Can I talk to him?'

'Oh, hang on a moment, I'll just lock up here and walk all the way over to his hall and up to the second floor and knock on his cell to see if he minds being interrupted.'

'Thank you so much.'

'What kind of chocolates do you think he'd like on his pillow?'

'What?'

'This *is* the Glasgow Hilton.'

'Fuck you,' she said.

'What did you say?'

'Thank you,' she lied, like daughter like mother. 'Would you mind leaving him a message? Tell him I'm coming home. I'll visit him next week.'

After that, Cynthia gave Preston his first shot at a bong. He took one puff, sat back and said, 'I see. It feels like someone has stuffed your head with cotton wool then put you in warm water. Yes, I can feel the sensation. Out of control. Other worldly . . . ' He paused. 'I can't really see the attraction.'

Then Cynthia gave Preston his first shot at a woman.

They were in a small hotel room on the

outskirts of Cairo. There was only one room
— 'Don't worry, I won't eat you!' Cynthia
had said, knowing she wasn't lying. She
wouldn't eat him. But he would most
certainly eat her.

'Have you seen one before?' she asked,
assuming the answer would be no. Despite his
stunning looks, she had never met such a
doofus in her life.

'Online,' he said. Vaginas were a bit like
dope to him. Didn't really understand the
attraction. Indeed, he found some of them
downright ugly — outies that you might
feed a peanut. However, he felt he should
become familiar with them, and with sex,
in the same way that he'd felt he should
try olives aged nine. He was glad he had
tried the olives. The bitter mites had tingled
a reminder in his mouth for an hour and a
half afterwards.

Cynthia dropped her hippy skirt to the
floor and stood before him. She had no pants
on. Preston stood and stared at her, not
moving.

'Why do you shave?' he asked. He was
trembling a little. It was more intriguing than
olives.

'It's nicer,' she answered. 'Don't you
think?'

'Not sure. I'd have to see it hairy to make a

concrete decision.'

'You'd have to wait a week or two.'

'I don't have a week or two,' he said. 'May I touch?'

'I insist.' Cynthia was turned on by his politely freakish behaviour. It made everything Preston was looking at swell.

He moved closer and brushed his index finger against her shaved pubic bone. It felt like a prickly elbow. It didn't scare him. But he had no compulsion to merge with it in any way.

He stood, walked to the basin, and began washing his hands.

'You can kiss it if you like,' Cynthia said, slightly annoyed. What was he doing?

'Thank you, but no,' he said, drying his hands. 'I'm tired. We have a big journey tomorrow.'

Cynthia put her skirt on. She had never been humiliated like this before, the little shit. She'd tell Heath. He'd be very angry.

* * *

The following day they boarded the flight to London. Preston flipped the pages of a book on the journey.

'Why don't you actually read it?' Cynthia asked, trying hard not to notice that the towns below were shaped exactly like syringes.

'I am,' he said.

'Crap.'

'Test me,' he said, handing her the book. It was called *Understanding Power: The Indispensable Noam Chomsky*.

Cynthia read the first page of the first chapter. It took her several minutes. She couldn't understand any of it, wouldn't manage to frame a question if he paid her.

'What's the first line?' she asked.

'Noam Chomsky is Institute Professor in the Department of Linguistics and Philosophy at MIT, Boston,' he said.

Smart arse, Cynthia thought, reading the *very* first words. She handed him the book and looked at the syringe-shaped clouds. Uncanny.

19

Linda and Will hadn't spoken for a fortnight. He said he'd call her when he got back from visiting Heath in Manchester, but he hadn't. He hadn't even been tempted, to be honest. After years of friendship, coupled with the occasional masturbatory fantasy, he was disappointed to find the actuality second rate and extremely painful. Instead of ringing her, he'd hidden himself inside the house — bar trips to the dialysis unit — and prayed that the following miracles would happen:

That the private detective would find Cynthia.

That Cynthia would agree to donate her perfect-in-every-way kidney.

That he would do the same.

And both girls would stop fading away as they were, the spirit and the life draining from their faces and bodies, and be all right.

None of these things had happened and now, two weeks after the wooden spoon to balls incident, Will was unexpectedly excited by her phone message. Georgie had fled the house after hearing it on loudspeaker, taking his mobile with her. He didn't have Linda's cell number written down, so he dialled her home number immediately, planning to hang up if her husband answered. Luckily, he didn't. She came over straight away.

'About the other night.' Will finished pouring Linda a large glass of red wine and handed it to her. He was about to ask her if being hit was a deal breaker. She misunderstood.

'Oh no, you're not getting away that easily,' she said. '*'About the other night!*' i.e., 'Thanks for the shag, Linda, now flick off to your wanker husband.' You left two weeks ago saying you'd call me and you never did. I've been at home trying to get rid of the arsehole, waiting for you to call. So let me tell you about 'the other night'. I needed it. I wanted it. And I'm going to have it again. I'm not going away. I'm not going anywhere. And you're going to hold me. I said fucking hold me, Will.'

★   ★   ★

After three more glasses of wine, Linda explained the farcical situation at home. Her husband, an arrogant pain in the arse prior to being caught red-handed, had taken to his knees. 'Literally,' Linda said. 'He does everything on his knees. You should see him

123

mowing the lawn. At dinner I can only see his hair. I had to tell the kids he'd injured his feet in a team-building canoeing accident.'

'Does he know about . . . ' Will stopped short of the *us* word.

'Fuck, no. This is too good. I'm enjoying it.'

Will didn't need to ask for an explanation — he'd been around housewives long enough to understand Linda's way of thinking. She liked her life. She liked the house and the holidays and the fact that her husband was away most of the time and that she could slag him off non-stop to her friends. It suited her. A lover was icing on the cake. Will didn't have the energy to work out his own thinking on the matter. He just wanted physical contact with someone.

It wasn't as bad as last time. No wooden spoons. But Linda was very demanding (On the chair, Still . . . Still . . . Edge of the bed . . . Still. Now you can move. Faster, *faster*. Out. Hand. Not there. No. Oh, you numbskull, there! I said *there*!) and Will really didn't feel like being bossed around. During the sixty minutes of precisely choreographed acrobatics all Will could think about was how long it might take before she'd finish.

Finally, Linda gave an ugly groan and slid off him.

The clock was ticking, Will thought, wiping sweat and other fluids from his chest with a tissue. He'd give the private detective one more week, then move on.

He was tired. He wanted to go to the toilet. If he asked her to leave, would she hurt him again?

20

When Cynthia and Preston arrived at Glasgow Airport, the rain moaned at them, as Cynthia recalled it had always done in this city — *See you*, the rain seemed to say, *I wet you weakly with my constant dribble.*

'You have one hour and fifty minutes,' she said to Preston. 'You're going to give me money for a room at the Marriott — I'll check in as Cynthia Jones. Get a move on! You now have one hour and forty-nine minutes.'

Preston had always managed the goals he set himself. He had never bought heroin, but it couldn't be hard in Glasgow, could it? He asked the taxi driver to drop him off on the edge of the Gorbals, donned a baseball cap and left Cynthia to continue on to her city-centre hotel.

Hmm, he thought, wandering past the new-build shops and eyeing each person he saw: single mother, car thief maybe, prostitute, social worker, social worker, social worker, kids dodging school . . . where were all the drug dealers? Perhaps this was the rejuvenated part — indeed, a high-rise apartment block had recently been blown to smithereens across the way, and privately owned flats lined several streets in the vicinity of the shopping area. He continued on. Drugs, surely, must still be readily available in the Gorbals, the famous, dangerous, dirty, poverty-stricken Gorbals.

He made his way past the health centre, the housing office, the social-work office, and then into a two-block by two-block wasteland where most of the buildings had been demolished. Ha, he thought, spotting a group of young neds hovering in front of one of the remaining buildings. He smiled and made his way over to do some shopping.

All five boys were around eighteen years old. The pack uniform was hooded cagoules and jeans. They spoke loudly to each other in rough accents Preston found difficult to understand. As he got nearer, he managed to recognise two words — gay and fucker.

'Hello,' Preston said, 'and how are you all?'

Another word this time: cunt.

'I'm just wondering if you have any gear.' Preston felt proud of himself. He was proving himself to be exceedingly street.

'Who's asking?'

'Preston MacMillan,' he answered, without thinking twice about the fact that he'd given his real name. These boys would never talk to

127

the police. They were on the same side.

'Whatchawanin?' The tallest of the five asked.

'Two bags of heroin, please,' he answered.

The boy gestured for Preston to follow him. As he did so, he realised they had all been standing at the front of the police station. Maybe they figured it was safer there. Or maybe they preferred not to have to walk too far once arrested.

Preston and the tall boy walked past a beautiful old chapel, over more wasteland and into the foyer of a high-rise building. There were CCTV cameras in the foyer. He kept his head down, cap obscuring his face, but wasn't too worried, really. Even if his face was visible, how would he ever be traced? The police had never photographed him or taken his fingerprints.

The boy pressed a button, waited for the lift and they got inside.

'So, have you lived here long?' Preston asked as the elevator elevated at snail's pace.

'Aye,' said the boy.

'Its nice to see they're doing the place up,' Preston said, now all out of chit-chat. He stared at the elevator buttons for several minutes before it finally crunched to a halt at the sixteenth floor. Maybe, Preston thought to himself, they made the lifts especially slow to help the unemployed fill their time. Or maybe it kept them off the streets longer.

The boy had a flat to the left. It had amazing views and was surprisingly well furnished. He's poor, Preston thought to himself, but his television is enormous. Maybe he stole it. Or maybe he's rich from selling gear.

'Here,' the boy said, returning from the bedroom with two bags of heroin. 'It's pure uncut shit, best there is, so be careful. A hunnert an' fifty quid.'

'Excellent,' Preston said, not realising that the street value of these bags was actually twenty pounds. Preston's ignorance made the boy's eyes twinkle. They twinkled tenfold as Preston took out his wallet, counted out £150 and handed it to him, another £500 and several credit cards visible inside the wallet.

It was pretty quick, what happened next. When Preston deconstructed it later, it reminded him of a scene from *Reservoir Dogs*:

Boy asks Preston to hand him the fuckin' wallet.
Preston enquires as to why.
Boy says Just fuckin gees it.
Preston says No.

Boy takes knife from back pocket and points it at Preston's neck.

Preston tries to run away.

Boy grabs Preston's arm before he gets to the door and twists it behind his back.

Preston says Ow!

Boy presses knife against Preston's neck.

Preston, feeling the point of the knife pierce his skin, uses all his strength to turn around, kick boy in the nuts and grab the knife.

Boy lunges towards Preston's neck with strangler's hands and vicious snarl.

Preston realises the knife he is holding is now halfway inside boy's chest.

Preston says Sorry, oh God, sorry, it was an accident.

Boy falls to the ground.

Preston no longer holds knife. Knife is now poking out of chest of boy who is lying on floor making choking sounds.

Then no sounds.

Preston checks if boy is breathing, says Shit, turns and runs down sixteen flights of stairs.

With two bags of heroin in his freshly murderous little hand.

Maybe he's not dead, Preston thought, head down.

Or maybe he is.

If he is, he thought, they would never suspect a seventeen-year-old boy genius from the trendy West End. And they had nothing on him, anyway. Some CCTV of his baseball cap perhaps, face obscured. Plus, he told himself, this was a disorganised crime, a gangland crime. He simply did not fit the profile. Walking determinedly towards the main road, Preston threw his cap in a bin and hailed a taxi.

21

As soon as I heard the message from the detective agency on Dads mobile I raced outside and returned the call. There was no answer on his mobile, so I left a message.

'This is Mr Marion's daughter returning your call,' I said. 'Call my father's number as soon as you can.'

I decided to have a drink while I was waiting.

* * *

It was a long wait. I woke the following afternoon in the back seat of a car. Some guy was half naked in the front. Who was he? He was old, twenty-five at least. While I was searching for my top, Dad's mobile rang. I grabbed it from my jeans pocket.

'Mr Marion?' came that voice again.

'This is his daughter,' I said.

'Georgie or Kay?'

'Georgie. Where are you? Is she with you?'

'She is, yes, but . . . it's complicated.'

'I know it's fucking complicated. Tell me where you are.'

'I'm in Room 234 at the Marriott, in town.'

The old half-naked guy took ages to work out how to drive his car. He was still drunk, I suppose. In the end, I kicked him out of the driver's seat and did it for him. Twenty minutes later, I stopped at the front of the Marriott hotel and opened the car door.

'Hey! You said you wanted my number,' he said.

'What's your name?' I asked.

'David.'

'I'm never going to fall in love with you, David,' I said, slamming the door behind me.

★ ★ ★

I ran up to the second floor and along the horror-film corridor. Taking a deep breath, I knocked on room 234.

'You?' I said. I'd seen this guy before — at the Bothy. He'd stared at me all night when I was there with Reece. He still had his sunglasses on, the drop-dead gorgeous wanker.

'Georgie? Don't come in just yet. Let me fill you in first.'

'Get out of my way,' I said, pushing past him and entering the hotel room.

There was no one on the bed. 'Mum?' I

said, nerve ends scratching as I looked around the room.

'Where is she?' I asked the sunglasses guy.

'In the bathroom. I came back and it was locked. I can't get it open.'

I tried the door. It was stuck.

The movie star with the sunglasses was saying, 'Oh no, I do hope she's all right.'

I had to kick it three times before it opened. And there she was, lying on the floor. I'd imagined her often. I'd even scanned one of our old photos onto the computer and downloaded an ageing device to see how she might have changed over the years, like they do for missing kids. On the computer, she looked the same as she had but with lines. In real life, here, now, on the bathroom floor, she looked like an emaciated wretch. There was nothing left of the woman in our photo albums.

'Mum?' I said, moving towards her, kneeling beside her, touching her hand. It was an elderly hand, my mum's; veined and liver-spotted and thin-skinned. Still, I was holding it, and it felt glorious.

'Mum?' I said, touching a cheek that felt not so different from her hand. Too much sun, maybe. 'Mum, I'm here.'

I don't know how long it took for me to notice the syringe beside her. Two seconds less than it took for me to notice the cloth tied around her arm.

'Mum!' I said more loudly, gently shaking her shoulders.

All the while, the sunglassed movie star had been saying the same thing over and over. I heard it now.

'Please tell me she's not dead. Please tell me she's not dead.'

22

'Is she breathing?' the sunglasses guy said. He was passing on instructions from the 999 operator.

'I don't know.' Turns out I was one of those dumb arses who cry in emergencies.

'She says she doesn't know . . . ' the guy relayed my words . . . and came back at me with an instruction. 'Put your cheek against her mouth.'

'What?'

'Put your cheek against her mouth and see if you can feel anything.'

'I can't feel anything.'

'She can't feel anything . . . ' He paused. 'Okay, put her on her back.'

'She is already.'

'She's on her back . . . ' he said to the operator, listened to the response, then said, 'Check there's nothing in her mouth.'

I put my finger inside my mother's mouth. It was warm. That'd be good news, wouldn't it? 'It's warm!' I said.

'Is her tongue there?'

'Yes.' I thought it was a stupid question but felt it best to answer. Where the hell else would it be? Of course later on I realised they wanted to know if she'd swallowed it.

'Her tongue's in her mouth . . . Georgie, stop crying. Georgie, listen to what I'm saying . . . Put the ball of one palm on top of the other and place them in between her boobs.'

Did the sunglasses guy really say *boobs*? At a time like this? Surely the operator didn't say *boobs*?

'Yes, she's doing that . . . Now press quite hard each time I count . . . You're gonna count to six hundred, okay? The ambulance is on its way.'

'One . . . two . . . ' Preston said. I couldn't seem to do as he asked . . . 'Three . . . four . . . You have to count out loud . . . Five . . . six . . . Georgie, count out loud! Nine . . . ten . . . Count out loud! No, she's not counting . . . He says *count*!'

I kept forgetting to count out loud. I couldn't stop crying. Would I save her? Would she live? 'Please live! Okay . . . eleven . . . twelve . . . Oh God.'

'Count out loud!' The sunglasses guy yelled.

'Thirteen . . . fourteen . . . Oh God. Oh no. Oh please!'

★　★　★

I don't recall what number I was at when they arrived. Not sure I got far beyond

137

fourteen. I was pretty hopeless at following instructions. It must have driven the sunglasses guy mad.

'My name is Preston,' he said. We were in the back of the ambulance. She was breathing. Maybe she had been all along. Maybe I pounded on her chest for no reason.

'Was it heroin?' I asked.

He shrugged his shoulders. The paramedic answered for me. 'The stuff on the street's too pure at the moment. We've had five deaths in the last week. Your friend was lucky.'

Friend? Is that what we looked like? 'She's my mother,' I said, squeezing her aged hand as we bumped towards Accident and Emergency.

'Preston, were you with her when this happened?' I asked.

'No. She asked me to leave her alone for a while. I went for a coffee, came back later and, well, you know the rest.'

'Will you do me a favour?' I asked. 'Don't ring Dad yet. I want to be the one who's with her when she wakes.'

★   ★   ★

Reece was on duty, and he managed to set up a portable dialysis unit in the bed next to my mother's. So Alfred bubbled beside me as I watched her. When she woke, I told myself, I wanted the first thing she saw to be me, her daughter. I hated that she'd see me this way, stuck with my Alfred, pathetic, immobile, sickly, but I had no choice. I barely blinked the whole time, afraid that I would miss the moment when she opened her eyes. She would be so overwhelmed. She would take a while to recognise me, a couple of seconds or so, I guessed. Then it would hit her, bang. That's my daughter, my beautiful daughter, Georgie, and she would smile and say my name . . . Georgie.

I was thinking all this when she opened her eyes and looked at me, just as I imagined. She squinted. These were the two seconds it would take for her to recognise me. Just as the time I had allocated for this came to an end, she leant over the bed and puked.

'Nurse! Nurse!' she yelled. Her voice was high pitched and whiny. I didn't expect her voice to be squeaky. Dad didn't know this, but years ago I found some of the uncut films he'd made of her singing. Her singing voice was husky, nothing like this.

'Get the fucking nurse and stop gawking, will you! Can you not see I'm fucking dying here!'

This request was for me, her beloved daughter. I pressed the buzzer beside me, watching as she sat up, wiped her mouth and repeatedly pressed her own buzzer with a thin angry finger.

My face didn't usually go hot in difficult situations. I got angry a lot, but the physical symptoms were quickly released by yelling or hitting something. This time, with no such release, the anger — or was it surprise — made its way to my face. Even my eyebrows were burning.

'Mrs Marion,' the doctor said. He and a nurse had arrived. 'You're a very lucky woman. You could have died.'

'I need to get out of here,' she said.

'Not today. We're in the middle of running some tests and we want to keep an eye on you.'

'But I have to get out of here. It's very important. There's somebody I have to see.'

My eyebrows cooled slightly. I smiled. Just as I thought, she was desperate to see us.

'You need to get some rest. If there's somebody I can ring for you, please tell me,' the nurse said.

'Just leave me alone,' she answered, then coughed, then rasped, then coughed again.

When they left the room, my mum sat up and attempted to get off the bed. Her hands and legs were shaking. She grimaced every time she moved. I watched as she put her feet

140

on the ground and opened the small bedside unit with her clothing inside.

'Are you going?' I said gently. Would she recognise my voice?

'Mind your own business.'

'Sorry,' I said, 'I was just wondering if there's something I can do to help. You said you have to see somebody. Is it somebody important?'

She'd taken off the gown and was trying to put on her jeans. Her hip bones jutted out above the low waist. I could see her ribs. She had a greyish bra on, but she didn't need it. She stood, zipped her jeans and pulled on a long colourful T-shirt dress. 'You really want to help?' she said.

'Yeah.'

'Then give me twenty quid and fuck off.'

23

While Georgie dealt with her illness by ignoring it as best she could (using alcohol and sex wherever possible), Kay was not dealing with it at all. She couldn't concentrate. Her exams were in a week, and she didn't understand any of the notes she'd taken before her body had caved in. *What does that line read?* she wondered, staring at the chemistry book in front of her. *It's all blurry.*

She knew she was seriously ill well before Georgie found out. She'd been nauseous and tired and unable to pee for a long time. Her father had always said she was a healthy child — three days off school in six years — but this wasn't really the case. Kay just got on with it. Walked to school with a raging headache. Played hockey with a throat infection. Did the shopping with a PMT depression. Studied hard with kidney disease.

As Kay sat in the dialysis unit, books laid out on the desk in front of her, she realised she could no longer ignore this. It was a bastard. She'd been forgetting to take her medication, forgetting to eat properly. She'd fail at this rate. And she no longer cared, to be honest.

No longer day-dreamed about her orchestra friend, Graham, suddenly kissing her, taking her by surprise, after a long build-up of sexual tension. What was the point of hope, the future, love, when she was disappearing towards death?

'Evie?' she said to the woman dialysing next to her. 'Can you call the nurse for me?'

'Sorry, dear?' Evie took her earphones out. She'd been watching one of her Catherine Cookson adaptations. 'What is it, love?' she asked Kay.

'Could you call the nurse for me?'

'Of course. NURSE!' Evie yelled with surprising strength. 'Nurse! Little Kay's not feeling too well.'

Where was Georgie? She should be here, Kay thought. *What does that line read? It's all wobbly. Oh, I am really sick,* she thought. *I am really, really sick. Georgie! Dad!*

And now I'm on the floor.

Samuel, dialysing opposite, latest Stieg Larsson thriller in hand, watched as Kay fell.

Little bitch, he said to himself. *She'll probably get one now. And it's my turn. See if she gets one, I'm going to my MP again.*

24

'I need more money,' Cynthia said into the payphone on Sauchiehall Street. She'd had to stagger for at least a mile to find a phone booth — they were pretty much extinct these days. The girl in the hospital had refused to give her twenty pounds, the obnoxious goth. Who did she think she was, anyway? What did she say again? 'Were you always a total cunt? Maybe you were. Maybe you were always a total cunt.' Sickly wee gobshite.

Without the twenty, Cynthia was in a pickle. She needed stuff, now. Some for her, some for Heath, and she needed travel expenses and a contingency fund. 'I won't see Will till you give me more money,' she said to Preston.

Preston, sitting in his office — not studying for maths as his mother thought but reading *War and Peace* for the second time — was pleased to hear from her. In the hospital two hours earlier, he'd gone out to get coffees for himself and Georgie — ah, Georgie — and when he came back, Cynthia had disappeared.

'Where is she?' Preston had asked his latest obsession.

'Who gives a fuck?' Georgie said. She'd been crying.

'Have you told your father I found her yet?'

'No,' she replied.

'Listen, I'll find her, okay? I'll sort this out.'

'I wouldn't bother,' Georgie said.

After sneakily retrieving one of Georgie's used nicotine chewing gums from the bin, Preston went home to think about his next step. He rolled the small ball of grey gum in his finger as he talked to Cynthia on the phone. It wasn't an ideal memento, but it would do for now. He liked that Georgie's saliva was mixed in with it.

'Where are you?' he asked Cynthia. 'Where can I meet you?' She suggested the Glasgow Film Theatre, in an hour.

★　★　★

Preston coped very well with stress. In the last twelve hours, he'd bought drugs, killed a man and helped save a woman's life. In the last two weeks he'd tracked down a missing person across two continents and fallen in love. As he walked from his West End flat toward the city centre, he realised that it was this last event which had tested him most. After getting the gig with Will Marion, he'd studied the family for some time. Preparation was the key to a successful project, he thought, and this meant knowing your client. So the very first thing he'd done was watch the family from a tree in their back garden. It was a lovely house on a street of lovely houses. Two storeys and a high pitched roof above a loft that most neighbours had converted into a bedroom. The gardens were well tended with hedges separating the long narrow strips of grass. The bins were lined neatly behind garages in the lane. This was a middle-class community where people followed rules and kept up with the MacTavishes. The three times he'd watched the house, he'd camouflaged himself in the tree by the back gate by wearing brown corduroy trousers and a brown jumper. He waited till it was dark, climbed the back gate, pulled himself up into the tree just inside the back garden and clung to the trunk as closely as possible. The first time, all blinds bar the one in the kitchen were closed, so he spent several hours watching the goings on in this one room. At 10 p.m. Will made three full-cream-milk hot chocolates and carried them out of the room. To the television room perhaps? Or to the bedrooms? At 10.30 Georgie helped herself to some cornflakes and ate them at the kitchen table. At 11.30 p.m. Kay got a glass of water and then turned off the light. At 12.30 Georgie sat at

146

the kitchen bench in the dark and stared at the fridge for twenty minutes.

The second time was the best. The upstairs bedroom blind was open. At 11.30 Georgie lay on her bed staring at the ceiling. At 11.40 she stood and looked at herself in the mirror. She was wearing jeans and a black sleeveless T-shirt. She began crying. She watched herself cry, not moving her hands to wipe tears or blow nose. She stood there, crying at herself. At 11.50 she took off her T-shirt and turned to the back garden (Had she seen him? Had she wanted him to see her?) and then — bugger — she closed the blinds.

The third time, the bathroom window was open. At 10.30 Kay cleaned her teeth. At 11.00 Will yelled: 'I'm on the toilet!' (The whole street must have heard him!) At 11.20 Georgie brushed her teeth. She did it very thoroughly, with an electric toothbrush. He wondered if she timed it with an egg timer.

He followed Georgie the day after the T-shirt incident. Watched her get in the car with her father. Watched her walk out of the hospital several hours later, pale and weak. Watched her go to a pub and flirt with some flabby guy.

She was beautiful.

Kind of wild in the eye. Kind of raw and angry.

Perfect.

He was in Sauchiehall Street, the nicotine gum now hard between his thumb and index finger. He missed the moisture. When moist, it had, in fact, turned out to be the perfect memento. He'd need a replacement.

As he turned into Rose Street and walked up the steep hill towards the cinema, he saw Cynthia sitting cross-legged on the ground outside, smoking a fag and looking annoyed. 'About time!' she said, standing to greet him. 'You got the money?'

'I'll need to okay it with my client,' Preston said.

If Cynthia had felt stronger, she would have refused this condition. But she was itchy and in need. 'Whatever,' she said. 'Just hurry.'

* * *

The phone rang twice before Georgie picked it up.

'Can I speak to your father, Georgie?' Preston said.

'What about?'

'It's confidential, I'm afraid.' Preston could hear a man talking in the background. His words were muffled for a moment — 'Give

148

me that! Give me the phone!' — and then clear as a bell.

'Hello, is this Preston?'

Oh bugger, they all knew his real name now. 'Yes. Did your daughter fill you in on what's been happening?'

'She did . . . finally.'

'I'm with Cynthia now. She wants more money. She says if she gets it she'll talk with you tomorrow.'

'How much?' Will asked.

'How much?' Preston relayed the question to a shaky, drawn Cynthia.

Mmm. Cynthia thought. How much? Was he still in the big house his daddy bought? Did his daddy still pay him ridiculous wages for a ridiculous job?

'A thousand,' she said, nervous that she had either started too high or too low.

'She wants a thousand pounds,' Preston said to Will.

'Tell her if she comes to the hospital right now, I'll give her two thousand.'

25

Turns out Kay was sicker than me. How had I not noticed? As I sat beside her bed, holding her hand and looking at her pretty, innocent face, I realised that she wasn't yellow like me, so much as deathly grey. How long had she been this colour? What a crap self-centred pain in the arse of a sister I'd been to not notice. All I'd thought about was me, assuming she was all right because she always said she was.

She was asleep when the phone rang.

'Tell her if she comes now, I'll give her two thousand,' my father had said. Where the hell was he going to get that? I knew the state he was in financially. The bank had been ringing constantly. Credit-card firms had been leaving messages every day. He had no job and wasn't even looking for one. He spent his time fetching and ferrying for us and trying not to cry.

'Is she coming?' I asked him.

'Yes.'

'Where are you going to get the money?'

'I dunno. Got any ideas?'

'Yeah. Actually I have.'

My father was crying now. He was kissing Kay's grey hand, tears streaming down his face. He was a mess. He didn't have the means or the strength of character to help Kay.

I was certain I did.

★   ★   ★

The time on the digital clock on the desk outside Kay's room didn't appear to work. A new minute flashed on the screen once every ten minutes, or so it seemed. My father and I looked at each other every now and again, then looked away abruptly, both of us knowing there was nothing to say, and nothing to do but watch the digital clock on the desk outside the room.

Across the corridor from Kay, a little girl of about nine was lying in bed. Her left eye was swollen to the size of a tennis ball. Some kind of scary infection by the looks. She had a drip in her arm. Her mother sat on her bed reading her a story. It was *Ping!*, I think, featuring a whole bunch of Chinese ducks. The girl had a tiny smile on her face. Suddenly, a man knocked on their door. 'Yoo hoo!' he said, smiling broadly as he sat on the other side of the bed. He kissed the girl on the top of her head and said, 'How's my beautiful brave girl? Is her every need being catered for?' He put cheese dippers and baked crisps and fruit smoothies and two new books on the bedside table, then sat down.

They linked hands — mother and father, father and daughter, daughter and mother. That's what it should be like in this room, I thought. When she walks in, it should be exactly like that. Oozing comfortable love. Since seeing my mother in hospital earlier that day, I realised that was never going to happen because my mother had turned out to be a total waste of space.

'What are you thinking?' Dad asked. What an irritating question. He always asked me that.

'Nothing,' I said.

'When you saw her . . . ' he said, 'what . . . what was she like?'

'She was shorter than I expected,' I said.

'Really? Hmm. Shorter.' He paused for a while but was unable to stop himself from attempting to fill the time with small talk. 'How old is Preston?' he asked. 'He sounded like a kid on the phone.'

'Seventeen,' I said.

Dad sighed out loud and shook his head. 'Really! Seventeen years old?'

Forty minutes had passed. Kay was still asleep. Dad and I had taken to pacing the room and checking ourselves in the mirror. My lips looked thin. Dad needed to moisturise. I was pacing and he was peering when Preston came in. Dad and I froze.

'She's nervous,' he said. 'She's in the waiting room. She asked me if I could take her the money first, to make sure.'

'What does she want the money for?' Dad asked.

'She didn't say.'

'How did you get her to fly back?'

'I promised her drugs.'

'She wants more drugs, doesn't she?'

'I think so.'

'Is she going to bugger off or is she going to help us? What guarantee do we have?'

'I don't know.'

'Is she still with Heath?'

'I think so.'

'Has she seen him?'

'Not yet.'

That was enough! I pushed past Preston and walked down the corridor and into the reception area. 'Where's the waiting room?' I asked the nurse at the desk.

'First left, go to the end of the hall, through the double doors, turn right, go down the stairs and it's the second on your right.'

I decided not to listen halfway through. Being female, I would stop and ask again.

'Where's the waiting room?' I said after getting to the double doors.

'Down that way, there's a sign' the doctor said.

When I walked in, she was drinking a can of Irn Bru on a plastic chair and reading *Red* magazine. How could she read a fucking magazine now?

'So what did you figure? We're worth a thousand each?' I said.

It was her turn to freeze. 'You again? Who are you?' she said.

'I'm Georgie Marion. You might remember me. I used to call you Mummy.'

To my surprise, she broke into an immediate hysteria which involved holding her head in her hands, rocking back and forth, sobbing like a baby and saying my name over and over. This totally scuppered my plan, which was:

a) to tell her to go fuck herself if she thought we'd pay her anything,

b) to tell her to go fuck herself if she played the 'I'm sick. I can't help it' card.

'That's bullshit,' I was going to say. 'See, I do have a disease. And so does Kay. We didn't choose to have it. We didn't inject it into our arms or sniff it up our noses. And we can't decide to not have it. You, on the other hand, have chosen. You have chosen to be a selfish waste-of-space junkie and now you are going to choose to save your daughter.'

Then I was going to haul her to her feet and drag her, kicking and screaming, into Kay's room, where the sight of her poor beautiful daughter would force her to help.

But she was crying her eyes out. She was saying my name over and over. 'Oh my God, Georgie, Georgie, my Georgie.'

'We're not going to give you any money,' I said.

'Of course, of course, I'm sorry,' she said, wiping her face with her sleeve, convulsing with tears. 'I don't know what I was thinking . . . My head's all over the place . . . You are so grown up.'

I grabbed her hand and helped her to her feet. 'Come and meet your other daughter.'

26

It had been thirteen years since she left. Since Will had waited at the window of their marital home, expecting her to return from a simple trip to the shops. During those years, he'd gone through the usual stages — anger and denial and all that — and until the kids had fallen ill, he had probably been firmly rooted in acceptance. As he watched his lovely girl lying on the hospital bed beside him, he wondered if any of those old feelings would return. He doubted it because all he felt was worry for Kay and all he could think was how he could help her.

She wasn't coping well with dialysis. Perhaps he hadn't monitored her closely enough. Perhaps he hadn't noticed that she was studying too hard, or forgetting to take her medication, or eating poorly. He would do better from now on. And perhaps there was a longer-term solution in the waiting room.

No, in the corridor.

Standing before him in the doorway of this hospital room.

Was that her? Was that the woman he used to adore? The one he cried over for years? The one he thought was better than him? She was frail and old-looking, like an anorexic art teacher. He hated to admit such shallow thinking at this moment, but Cynthia was exceedingly unattractive. Had he really loved her once?

'We don't have the money,' Will said. He looked into the eyes he used to think were deep and saw nothing. 'We just have two very sick children.'

What she did next surprised him. She walked to the bed, took Kay's hand, kissed it, fell to her knees, and prayed . . . 'Dear God, let her be okay.' She then looked up at Will and Georgie, tears streaming: 'Of course I'll help. I'm not a bad person. I'm a good person. Of course I will.'

★ ★ ★

In the room opposite, the nine-year-old girl had fallen asleep. Her father had gone home. Her mother was putting water in the vase. After she'd filled it and placed it on the windowsill, she looked over into Kay's room and caught Will's eye. She smiled at him. They were in the same boat, were they not? A sick child surrounded by an abundance of comfortable love.

This illusion was interrupted by two things. First it was by Will, who said, 'Right, keep her here, Georgie. Don't let her out of your sight. I'll go get the doctor.'

And then by the doctor who had dealt with the girls since their diagnoses. Will knew where his office was. He'd sat in it many times, the last of which was when he'd asked not to be tested yet, not till he found another donor.

'William!' Mr Jamieson said as Will rushed through the door. 'Are you all right? I'm glad you're here. Sit down, sit down. I've been wanting to talk to you about your parents.' Mr Jamieson turned his Van Morrison CD down. 'Brown Eyed Girl' faded into the background.

'My parents?'

'They came in last week.'

'Really? I didn't know. That's not why I'm here . . . I have some amazing news.'

Mr Jamieson was taken aback by Will's urgent excitement, but he was an important *Mister*, so his news should go first. 'Sit down, take it easy. Relax.'

Will wouldn't sit down.

'They were tested, Will. They didn't want to get your hopes up, which is probably why you hadn't heard about it yet.'

'They were?' Will couldn't believe his ears. They'd done it.

'I'm afraid both have unsuitable tissue types. There were other considerations as well. Your mother in particular may not be healthy enough to withstand major surgery and recover completely. It's not good news. They can't be donors.'

Will's heart sank — this was option 2) in his notebook, gone.

But only for a moment. It didn't matter any more. 'I've found Cynthia,' he blurted. 'She's here. She's agreed to donate. How quickly can you test us both? We want the operations done as quickly as possible.'

'Mr Marion, calm down. I'd like you to take a seat, please.'

'I don't want to sit down. Didn't you hear me? She's here! She's said yes!'

Mr Jamieson walked slowly to the door, closed it, then walked even more slowly back to his desk. 'I suggest you sit down,' he said.

Will could feel the optimism dribbling out his ears. He flopped into a chair and said, 'What?'

'I treated your ex-wife yesterday. She'd overdosed on heroin.'

'And?'

'And . . . I need to speak to her before I speak to you.'

'Just tell me. What is it?'

'She used heroin for over fifteen years, Will. Do you know what that can do to your body?'

Will's neck lost its ability to hold up his head. As it dropped, all the air inside him came out.

'In addition to the effects of the drug itself, street heroin often contains toxic contaminants or additives that can clog the blood vessels leading to the lungs, liver, kidneys, or brain, causing permanent damage to vital organs.'

She'd gone and screwed up her fucking kidneys. The realisation slowed every sound and every movement. Small moans infiltrated his breathing.

'Will?' Mr Jamieson said, walking around his desk to perch himself on the front of it. He'd learnt this technique from his wife, an oncologist in the Beatson Clinic. 'You don't want to touch them,' she'd told him after her husband came home one night. He'd had a difficult session helping a patient explain to his family that he no longer wanted to dialyse — i.e. that he wanted to die. The wife had grabbed him and hugged him for four minutes. He had snot on his shoulder afterwards. 'But you need to show them you're human,' his wife explained. 'An

160

inch of bum on the desk edge and a sigh does the trick.'

Mr Jamieson sighed. 'I'm very sorry. We just have to wait for the right donors for your girls.'

'Of course.'

'Is there anything I can do?'

Will couldn't answer him. He couldn't even lift his head. Was he still breathing?

'Mr Marion? I'm afraid I have to get on now.'

'Of course,' Will said quietly, slowly standing and leaving the room.

★ ★ ★

Will's pace quickened as he retraced his steps back to Kay's room. He pushed the door open so hard that it frightened Georgie and Cynthia, and woke Kay.

'You useless bitch!' he yelled, moving towards the still-kneeling Cynthia. 'You fucking useless bitch!'

'Dad!' Georgie put herself in front of her father. He'd gone mad. He was going to kill her mother.

'Dad, stop!' Kay said weakly. 'What's going on? Who's this?' She pulled her hand from Cynthia's grasp. Who was this woman? Why was she kneeling at her bed? Why was she

161

holding her hand?

'This?' Will said pointing at Cynthia. 'This is the woman who abandoned you when you were three. This is the woman who wanted to screw a drug dealer rather than look after you. This is the woman who chose heroin and a thug over us. This . . . ' Will was still trying to get away from Georgie's stronghold. He wanted to hurt her. 'This is the woman who chose to screw up her organs. You screwed them up, Cynthia. They're useless to us. Get out of here. Go away. GET OUT OF HERE!'

Georgie released her grasp. She and Will stared at Cynthia, who was now sitting on the floor beside Kay. She'd stopped crying. She didn't realise it, but her face was unable to hide her true feelings. She could get out of here now. She'd offered, done the right thing, been unselfish — as she always had been — and now she could go and relieve some stress and talk to Heath. He'd make her feel better. She deserved to feel better. Should she stand up straight away? Or protest first?

'It can't be,' she was the kind of person to decide on the latter. 'I must be able to help.'

'You can't,' Will said. 'As ever, we're better off without you. Just go.'

She turned to Kay, who had said nothing. Kay's expression was kind, but no more than

162

that. She rolled onto her side so that Cynthia could no longer look at her. 'You were always the pretty one,' she said, touching Kay's hair.

Georgie bit her lip.

'I'll go, then,' Cynthia said.

The mother in the room opposite watched as Cynthia left the room. As it turned out, these two families had nothing in common.

27

For some reason, Will had skipped ahead to the fifth page of his notebook and was now writing on it.

There were many reasons for this, in fact.

First, he had phoned his parents to thank them for being tested. This is how the phone call went:

MOTHER MARION: Well, it's the least we could do. I'll put your father on.

FATHER MARION: We have the wrong tissue type, son.

WILL: What did you say?

FATHER MARION: I said we have the wrong tissue type, son.

WILL: I heard what you said.

FATHER MARION: Then why did you ask me to repeat it?

WILL: I'm fucking tired of you, Dad.

FATHER MARION: What did you say?

WILL: I said I'm fucking tired of you, Dad.

Will hung up.

Not long after the phone call, Will hit

Georgie. He'd done this a few times when she was younger. Usually a pathetic tut-tut to the hand which shocked her into submission and tears but punished him much more. He always felt so guilty and ashamed afterwards that he threw all parenting skills to the wind and gave Georgie whatever she wanted for at least a week, so long as she tried to forget what he had done. He'd never hit Kay. She'd never pressed his buttons the way Georgie had.

Somehow, corporal punishment had seemed less inappropriate when Georgie was much shorter than him. This evening, he had started a fight with virtually a grown woman — wrong in itself — but even more terrible considering the unwritten rule that children should never hit their parents back.

She'd pushed him to the limit again.

That old excuse.

She'd called him a failure.

No reason to threaten her . . . *One more word young lady!*

She'd said if it wasn't for him maybe Cynthia would never have turned to drugs.

Still not grounds to grab her and hold her against the kitchen wall with his arm.

If it wasn't for him, she would be healthy

and happy and Kay wouldn't be at death's door.

That was it. That was enough. How dare she?

★ ★ ★

It happened several hours ago, but his hand was still red from the connection with his daughter's face.

He began chanting a skipping-rope game the girls used to play when they were younger.

No missing a loop. If you do you'll get no soup. No excuses will be taken less you go to Doctor Bacon.

He was drunk, which was probably the second reason for his note-taking on page five of his jotter.

Georgie, he wrote in one column.

Kay, he wrote in the other.

Using his ruler, he drew a line down the middle.

He underlined the names with the ruler.

He made two columns under each name, headed *Pros* and *Cons*.

Before writing anything further, he took another swig from the second bottle of red wine he had opened that night. *Where was she?* he wondered. After the face slap, he had slid down the kitchen wall and cried like a baby. He hadn't seen or heard anything for several minutes. During that time, she must have left. He'd got up eventually and checked every room. She was no longer in the house. She'd left the front door open. She was somewhere else altogether. Where had she gone?

He returned to his work in progress . . . the pros and cons of Georgie Marion, sixteen years old.

The pros and cons of Kay Marion, also sixteen.

Where was Kay? In hospital still, resting as she had been instructed, with Mr Jamieson and the nurses taking better care of her than he had. Making sure she took her medication and that she ate properly and rested and would recover in time for her exams.

Will took the last swig from the bottle. The notebook was beckoning but he needed another bottle and a joint. He couldn't do this without dope.

Where was it?

When had he last had some? Years back, Linda had come over with a small bag. 'Here, Good Guy,' she'd said. 'You need to chill out.'

He rummaged through the filing cabinet in the corner of the room. Didn't he put it in the D file a few years back? Clever, hey? D for dope. Could've chosen G for grass or C for cannabis — the options were endless — but he'd gone for D all those years ago as nothing else in his life seemed to start with D. What in his life started with D? Hmm. Dry cleaning — who'd file anything about dry cleaning? And anyhow, none of his clothes required ironing, let alone dry cleaning. There was something in his life starting with D now, he thought. Death.

It wasn't in the D file.

Oh, that's right, he remembered. He'd moved his stash when he realised the girls might go in there for dance timetables and put it under M (for marijuana), where it would rest alongside mortgage documents that were of no interest whatsoever to them.

Aha! A small plastic pocket next to his latest mortgage reminder. It had one of those press-shut plastic seals at the top. It was still there, and inside was a small lump of greenery.

What was he doing? What had he just written down? Since the diagnosis, the option had been in the back of his mind, he supposed, in the same way that winning the lottery always had, or smashing Cynthia over the head with a large metal object had, but he never thought he would knowingly take it from the back and move it to the front, that he would let it travel to the pen in his hand so it would be written down in his notebook, that he would now be anaesthetising himself in order to consider it seriously. It was ridiculous. He should never have let the idea enter his mind at all. He should rip that page to shreds.

But what was he doing? The dope! Ah, there it was. He was on a roll to make a roll and would finish one thing at a time.

He had some tobacco in a pouch taped under his desk. And some papers in an old box filled with street maps of Glasgow, Arran and York (he'd taken the girls to York for a weekend three years earlier. It was pretty stressful. Georgie made it known that she found everything about the city boring).

Licking the papers and sticking them together felt nice, a ritual that had always soothed him.

Still, he should never have hit her.

He placed some of the dry tobacco on the paper then crumbled some of the stale weed on top of it, like pepper. He fashioned a roach from the corner of a box of multivitamins on his desk and rolled the neatest joint he had ever rolled.

Just like riding a bicycle.

28

That guy was following me. I'd known since the corner of Buchanan Street and Argyle Street but I didn't want to let on. He was about ten metres behind me now. Every time I turned my head slightly to the left or right, he stopped and pretended to look in a shop window. Either he wasn't very good at it or he didn't care if I saw him.

The cold air pinched at my left cheek. I hadn't looked, but I could feel the shape of my father's hand imprinted there. Prick. I should have hit him back. Why didn't I? Maybe because I'd never seen him so out of control. Oh, dull composed father of mine.

'Georgie, your mother is never coming back,' he'd said when I was three and again and again till I was ten. 'She likes bad things. We should count our blessings,' or some such shit.

'Georgie, you're sick, darling. You need dialysis.'

'I know the whole list thing is hard, but we need to be patient.'

For the first time ever, he completely lost it: yelling and screaming in the hospital,

170

trying to hit that wretched feral stray who was my mother. That's what happens when you store shit inside for a lifetime. It rots, then explodes.

It had been the most exhausting and upsetting day of my life. When I got back to the safe haven of my home, the last thing I needed was more crap. The fucking bully. I don't even know what I said that annoyed him so much that he whacked me on the head.

I was in front of the St Enoch Shopping Centre now. It was after midnight and the town was deserted bar the two of us. I'd been drinking since the slap, my usual response to stress, but the alcohol had merely numbed me a little, like it does when you have a cold. I needed something more. As I heard Preston's footsteps on the concrete behind me, I wondered if I might be able to have some fun with this. Hell, I needed some fun.

My mission to find love! It was at times like this that I turned to my newfound diversion from the facts of my life, which in twenty-four hours had increased by three million to the power of crap.

'Reece? Sorry to wake you,' I said. 'But I need to talk to someone.'

I walked all the way to his flat in the Merchant City. It was in one of those old warehouses that people think are trendy but are actually just old warehouses filled with poxy boxy flats. His was on the first floor.

I deliberately left the foyer door open, gently wedging a rock under it with my foot. On the first floor I snibbed the front door of Reece's flat before walking into the living room as he had instructed me to do over the intercom.

He had everything that I wanted ready: some more of that powder we'd had at the Bothy before it made me walk into a pillar, and his dick, somewhere under those godawful pyjamas.

I ingested the powder first, but my anger and adrenalin diffused it, as it had the alcohol.

'I need some more,' I said. 'That's doing nothing.'

Reece placed a small lump on his glass coffee table and cut at it with his Bank of Scotland card. He lined it up neatly for me and handed me a sawn-off straw.

'Do you mind if I get into something more comfortable?' he asked. I almost exhaled all the coke with my laugh. 'What could be more comfortable than those things?' I said, looking at his blue flannelette number.

'I'll just be a minute.'

I leant back into the sofa — black leather,

of course — and closed my eyes. Where was Preston? Had he come in yet? Where would he hide? I focused: my ears are bionical, oh yes they are, and they will seek you out!

Some whistling from the bedroom: Reece.

A tap dripping in the kitchen: the tap.

Nothing . . .

Nothing . . .

Whistle . . .

Tap . . .

Ah, there . . . amongst all that, a tiny cough. I waited . . . hggh hgggh, again . . . muffled this time. He'd probably put his hand over his mouth.

I waited, then opened my eyes and looked in the direction of the cough. Ha-ha. It had come from the hall cupboard, just outside the living room.

'Reece? Are you okay? Are you going to be long?'

'Just a couple of minutes!' he yelled.

'While you're in there, I'm going to the toilet!' I wanted to give Preston time to find a better hiding place. What would he see from the hall cupboard?

Alas, no wee. And while vodka and Coke and coke had done nothing to enhance my mood, it had certainly worked on my good health. Don't close your eyes, G, I said to myself. Close your eyes, and you're dead meat.

I wiped, although there was no need to, and entered the living room again.

'Reece!' I said, 'I'm back in the living room!'

'Just a minute!' he said. What on earth was he doing?

Standing in the middle of the living room, I looked carefully at the possibilities. Was Preston behind the dark grey curtains? (Who would choose dark grey curtains? Did Reece not have enough dark grey in his Glasgow life already?) I couldn't see a bulge . . . maybe Preston had decided it was too obvious.

I tiptoed over to the sofa. Perhaps he was lying behind it. But I didn't want to know for sure so I didn't peek. Not knowing added to the excitement.

Oh, and there was a bamboo screen, separating the dining table from the sofa/ television area. That'd be a good choice, I thought. Stand behind that. A bit risky, but there were clothes hanging over it so perhaps he could use those to disguise himself.

Reece was back.

'Oh my fudge, you look wonderful!' I said. He had changed into a nurse's outfit. Not the one he wore at work, mind — all sensible trousers and ironed shirt — but a PVC nursey number, with a zip all the way from the bottom to the top. The bottom only just hid his bits, which I feared may have been harnessed (or not) by a girl's thong. At the top, he wore a padded bra, probably with chicken-fillet inserts to enhance his cleavage. He had patterned white stockings (the kind with a seam down the back of the leg) and white high-heeled shoes (the kind a bride might wear).

On his head was a small nursey hat thing. Around his shoulders a stethoscope.

'How are you feeling this evening, Ms Marion?' Nurse Reece said. He had lipstick on. I have to admit, it suited him. Green wasn't the right colour eye shadow for him, though. Perhaps I'd tell him one day.

'I'm feeling very poorly,' I said, still trying to decide on the whereabouts of my stalker. 'I'm so glad you're here to help me, nurse. But my eyes can't cope with all this light.' I dimmed the lights down so far that — yes — I could now see the reflection of Preston's arm in the bay window. Not wanting Nurse Reece to see the same, I closed the grey curtains.

'What do you think is wrong with me?'

'I think you need a big cock in your cunt,' he said.

'Really?' I said. 'Is that it? All that work and

that's it? Straight onto the cock-in-cunt thing?'

He lifted the dress a little and there it was — the cock that he intended for my cunt.

'Oh yeah, baby.'

'Oh yeah, baby?' I repeated. 'Goddam it. Get down.'

'What?'

'Sit on the sofa. You're a bollocks nurse.' I slowly unzipped the dress all the way and took it off him. He looked hilarious dressed in nothing but stockings, heels and a hard on.

'Let me be the nurse,' I said. 'Kneel on the couch and do as I say.'

* * *

I do hope Preston appreciated all the effort I made. Bum high in the air, pointed right at his screen hiding place. Careful unveiling, not too much, not too soon. Cunning use of filthy talk that he could easily interpret as being just for him. Heels on no matter how tricky the position. After Reece had reached his *Code Red! Code Red! Code Red!* I locked myself and Reece in the bathroom long enough for Preston to exit the flat.

'I thought you said you were never going to fall in love with me,' Reece said as he lathered his pubic hair into a Santa beard. Mascara and green eye shadow was running down his chubby cheeks.

'I won't,' I said. 'Have you seen my pants?' God, Reece was gross naked. He wasn't overly fat, but he had man boobs. And his dick had shrivelled into the inch of gathered foreskin. Blah. I had to leave, forget the pants.

I would never fall in love with Reece.

No, but I might just do so with Preston.

29

If this was a film, Will thought, it would be a legal drama. He would be the logical, no-nonsense solicitor. He would gather evidence methodically and list his findings succinctly. Like most films, it would also be fiction, of course. He wasn't doing this for real. He was just drunk. Oh, and stoned. 'Photographs!' he said out loud. I'll start with those.

The dope was stale, but it had added a little something to the two bottles of wine he had now finished. He walked as a lawyer might towards the glass-fronted cabinet in the living room and ran his finger along the album spines as a lawyer might search for the correct legal journal in a law library. 'Ah, that's the one! Georgie . . . Aged One to Five. Kay, Aged One to Five.'

He returned to his desk, moved the table on his notebook to one side and opened the first page of Georgie's first photo album.

She didn't smile much. As a newborn, she screamed non-stop. Of the ten photos of her aged nought to one, she smiled in only one photograph. Will didn't remember the moment — she was around twelve months old, sitting on the green sofa in the back room, pointing at something and grinning. What had made her smile? The outside world? The television? Her mother?

Things looked even worse from two to five. Not crying, but serious to the point of angry. A downturned mouth, yes, a scowl, in every shot (even the one on the beach in Largs!), and watery eyes, as if she'd just stopped crying or was just about to start.

Hmm, what an unhappy kid. Was she born like this? Are some children born miserable?

He needed another bottle of wine before he could write the words. In the slim kitchen unit beside the cooker, there was one bottle left. He'd been drinking red, and this was white, but what the heck. He opened it, filled his large red-wine glass and returned to his desk with a weak-looking 'rosé'.

He also needed the kind of pen a solicitor in a legal drama might use. Not a bog standard biro, or the one with a fluffy green feather thing on top that Kay had given him aged seven, but a serious pen. There it was, the Kingsley Cosmopolitan Teal Green-Chrome Ballpen which Georgie had given him last Christmas (to 'Write an Oscar winning thriller!'). She hadn't noticed that he never wrote longhand. Who did nowadays? He'd never taken the pen out of its black case.

'My first note in the case against Georgie Marion,' Will garbled, 'is . . . '

In the GEORGIE/CONS column he wrote *Born unhappy and stayed that way*.

He should have written a pro first, he realised, guilt making its way through his drunken lawyerlyness. He quickly added *Cute* under her PROS.

'Now, let's look at exhibit two, Kay Marion, aged zero.' There she was, page one of her first photo album, smiling in the hospital just moments after she exited that woman's body. People say newborn babies don't smile, but look at that. No two ways about it.

Page three: laughing aged two as Rudolph the hamster crawls up her arm. Four: Giggling aged three on the swing in Rouken Glen Park.

Five: Grinning aged five at the dance rehearsal.

Will refilled his glass and added under KAY/PROS: *Born loving life and stayed that way*.

He knew he should write some cons and he did think very hard about this — as a lawyer would — but from the evidence on offer, there was nothing negative to say about Kay aged nought to five.

★ ★ ★

It was around three in the morning when he moved onto the next section. Had he ever been so off his head? Perhaps with Si in his late teens, when he rode his bicycle into an obnoxious man outside the pub and pedalled home to vomit into the laundry basket. What was he doing? Ah yes. New evidence was necessary for the five to ten section. It took him an hour of singing to Blondie's 'Denis Denis' to work out what.

School reports, in the filing cabinet, under S.

Georgie's comments were similar throughout her early school years: *Disruptive. Distracted. Poor attention span. Seems uninterested. Enjoys more creative work. Should work harder. Trouble socialising with other girls.*

Kay's were also consistent: *Excellent work. Progressing well. Works hard. Always interested and motivated. Gets on well with classmates.*

It was becoming difficult to write legibly,

but Will reminded himself that court cases are difficult and perseverance is the key to success:

GEORGIE/CON: *Finds it difficult to conform*
KAY/PRO: *Wants to fit in and does*
GEORGIE/PRO: *Creative*

He had written *Creative* last, once more a reaction to the guilt which was now niggling at him a little less than before. Why did Georgie find it so hard to fit in? School was always awful, uniforms were always stupid, organised activities were always a waste of her time, her friends were always talking about her behind her back and dumb bitches anyways.

Oh God, he was so pissed.

'Exhibits E and F for the girls aged ten to sixteen?' He knew what he needed straight away. He ran up the stairs, tripping twice along the way, and went into Georgie's room. He had to rummage through the two-foot pile of paperwork and make-up on her desk (not there), under her bed which was crammed with dirty clothes and presents he'd given her and she'd never used (not there), through her bookshelves which were lined with depressing literary fiction and books about the film industry (not there) and through her underwear drawer which housed inappropriately skimpy, lacy pants and bras and — oh God — is that what I think it is? Does she have one of those already? I thought it was only housewives who had those . . . Aha! There it is!

. . . Her diary.

Kay's journal was sitting neatly on her desk. Will grabbed it and returned to his office with both books.

He knew he shouldn't. He never had. But this was life or death. Oh no it wasn't. This was nonsense. Drink some water. You can't even stand up.

Will staggered to the bathroom and put his mouth under the tap. He glugged at the water for several minutes. He splashed his face. He looked in the mirror. 'This is life or death. They could both die. Or one of them might die.' His drunkenness had now reached the crying point. They could both die. Or one of them could die. What would he do without them? Who would he be without them?

Who would I be? Will fell to the floor and sobbed into the cold tiles. What would I do? Oh God, what would I do?

What was he thinking? Why wasn't he exhausting the other options before even thinking about drawing that stupid table in that stupid office? He lifted himself from the bathroom floor, wobbled back to the office — the water had sobered him only marginally — and fell into his chair.

Oh look, Kay's diary was on the desk. And it was open.

30

11 years old

Dear Monty,

When I grow up I'm going to get rich and give dad the money to make a movie. He'd make a great movie. Maybe a musical! Maybe I could be in it. I'm going to practise my acting and singing so I'm as good at it as Georgie. I'm going to save 10p out of my pocket money every week. I'll put it in a special 'movie' tin.

12 years old

Dear Monty,

Today I went to Loudoun Castle with Dad and Georgie. It was SO fun! I went on thirteen rides including the Black Pearl. Graham from second year was there and said hi to me. He is very good on the trombone. I wish Georgie had brought her jacket like I did. Then she might have been warm enough to enjoy it.

13 years old

Dear Monty,

I suppose it's normal for a teenager to be tired all the time. I don't like being a teenager. I want my energy back.

Graham from orchestra asked me out today. I said no. I like him but I'm too young for a boyfriend. Anyway, he's a mate and I don't want to ruin that.

I am so lucky! My Dad is the best Dad in the world. And my sister! Last night she slept on the floor in my room and held my hand all night because I felt nervous about exams. All night! Sometimes I have to pinch myself. I have the perfect family.

14 years old

Dear Monty,

I feel a bit drained today. Dad says I'm just doing too much as usual. I wonder if I should quit dancing. Or netball. Or flute. Or athletics. I don't want to quit anything.

I thought about her today. I tried my usual trick of stamping her out like a cigarette but it didn't work. I wish I could ask her about what to do.

All the other girls have done at least that and I feel left out. But I still don't want to go out with Graham. It doesn't make any sense to go out with him now.

Georgie says if I don't want to go out with Graham then I shouldn't. But she doesn't understand why I don't want to. She's so much cooler than me! I wish I could be more like her.

I'm just going to go and talk to Georgie.

15 years old

Dear Monty,

School is more fun than it used to be. The girls are much friendlier to me. I feel okay about being (reasonably!) clever. I think I'll be a physiotherapist when I grow up. I like working with people. And I'm good at biology.

I've stopped thinking about her. It's all too tiring. Graham has given up on me. I think he likes Sarah. Makes me feel really sad when I think of them getting together. Maybe I should've just gone for it. Y'know, I think I might be in love with him. Bethanay and Archie's mum from round the corner fancies dad. It's so obvious. She's a bit mad in the eye (screams at her kids like all the time), but I kind of wish he'd just go for it. He needs someone.

16 years old

Dear Monty,

I'm feeling pretty bad at the moment to be honest but a girl from the other unit got the call yesterday. She waited five years and now she's got it. So it can't be so bad can it? It'll all be okay, won't it?

Let it all be okay.

Will smiled as he wrote. She was a darling, this girl. An uncomplicated, kind darling. And what about Georgie? What a lovely sister she'd been. Had he not noticed this? She was always looking out for Kay, always there for

188

her — she held her hand all night! Oh!

GEORGIE/PRO: *A wonderful sister*

KAY/PRO: *Uncomplicated, kind darling*

KAY/PRO: *Has loads of interests — dancing, netball, flute etc.*

KAY/PRO: *Loves a boy called Graham (first I knew of it!)*

KAY/PRO: *Ambitious and hopeful — wants to be a physiotherapist*

KAY/PRO: *Loves me*

Kay loves me, Will thought. And Georgie is a wonderful, kind, sister. He was a lucky man to know them both.

He touched Georgie's diary. He had no idea what he might find inside. It made him a little scared. His hand was shaking. The diary opened somewhere in the middle, the first of several pages which had separate sheets stapled to it. He unfolded the first stapled sheet of paper and read:

Aged 12

Dear Mum,

I love you. I hope what I'm doing won't hurt you because it's not your fault that I can't take it any more. Life is something I'm not interested in.

189

Apparently this will not hurt me. I'll just fall asleep. When I do, I'll be thinking of you.

G

Will gasped and flicked forward — there was another piece of paper stapled to a page two-thirds of the way though the diary.

Aged 13

Dear Dad and Kay,

Goodbye. Please don't blame yourselves. It's me. I'm just not into being around.

G

And another, near the end . . .

Aged 15

Dad,

I'm going to kill myself. You'd be surprised how easy it is to get a gun. Sometimes you've gone on and on at me so much I swear I could use one on you. *I want this to hurt you. You deserve it.*

G

Will banged the diary shut. Before he could change his mind, he had written the following:

GEORGIE/CON: *Mean selfish horrible*

GEORGIE/CON: *Has no hope, no ambition, no kindness*

GEORGIE/CON: *Loves no one bar a woman who does not exist*

GEORGIE/CON: *Hates me*

GEORGIE/CON: *Hates everything*

GEORGIE/CON: *Has she bought a fucking gun? Jesus*

GEORGIE/CON: *Wants to die*

GEORGIE/CON: *Thought about killing me!*

He had never been so angry. Or so pissed. He threw his pen at the window. He bashed his fist at the desk. He growled, stood, punched the door of his office once, then again, again, until there was a hole in the door like the one he had punctured in the kitchen. And blood all over his hand.

'I see you've calmed down,' Georgie yelled from the hall.

* * *

191

God, God, God. Will raced to his desk, grabbed his notebook, tore the table from his book, ripped it in half, scrunched it into a tight ball, and shoved it in the top drawer of his desk. 'Georgie?' he said. 'I'm sorry! Georgie! Where are you, baby? I'm SO sorry! Where are you?' He walked out into the hall, looked in the kitchen, walked up the stairs and into her bedroom. She was sitting on the bed.

'Please forgive me!' Will said. 'I shouldn't have slapped you.'

'Assaulted me. I could call the police, you know. I could call ChildLine.'

'I shouldn't have assaulted you. Are you okay? Where have you been?'

'Around.'

'You're drunk,' Will said.

'So are you,' she replied. 'You should fix up that hand. Come . . . ' She walked her father to the bathroom and retrieved Savlon spray and plasters from the medicine cabinet.

They were silent for a moment, Will sitting on the edge of the bath, Georgie standing over him, washing, disinfecting, bandaging.

'I'm going to make everything all right,' Will said, the cut now tended to. 'I'm going to sort this out, my lovely girl.'

'Oh yeah?' she said, sitting on the edge of the bath next to him.

192

'Yeah.' Will touched Georgie on the cheek, not knowing if she would jerk to remove him the way she usually did, fobbing him off with a *Fuck off, Dad*. She didn't. She moved her face into his touch and smiled sadly at him. He smiled back, but neither lasted long. Within a second, both were crying.

'Please don't let me die!' she embraced him, sobbing. 'Dad! Daddy! Please don't let us die.'

31

The back of Heath's block edged the thick red brick wall that surrounded the prison. On the other side was a nondescript road. People often threw things over the wall into the yard, hoping their loved ones would be in position at the right time to catch their offerings (usually drugs, hidden in a variety of ways, which included inside dead rats).

Cynthia hoped Heath would be in the cell he'd been occupying one year earlier. She knew where to position herself so he could hear her dulcet tones through the grating in his wall.

It was after lights out. She would wake him. But he wouldn't mind.

'Heath Jones! I love you!' she yelled from the quiet road outside.

'Heath Jones, I fucking love you!' she yelled again. 'You are the love of my life! My name is Cynthia and I love Heath Jones. I love you, Heath!'

Heath woke immediately and jumped out of his bunk. Standing on tiptoes with his mouth touching the grating, he dribbled as he yelled ... 'Cynthia Marion, I love you!

Cynthia! Don't go away again! Wait for me! I love you, Cynthia! Sing to me!'

'Shut the fuck up,' his first-timer cellmate said from the top bunk. If he'd been properly conscious, he'd have thought twice about making such an objection.

Heath walked over to his bunk, pulled the novice to the ground and kicked him seven times, until he was unconscious.

★   ★   ★

Cynthia didn't leave. She sang songs she and Heath had written together for over half an hour, undeterred by objections from officers and inmates. Tired of singing to an unappreciative crowd (*Ya sound like a fuckin' cat!*), she lay on her coat and camped outside the front of the prison like a teen waiting for concert tickets. In the morning, she dragged herself from the doorway she'd taken shelter in and went inside to book a visit.

Within an hour they were sitting opposite each other in the visits room. Looking at them, you wouldn't know they loved each other more intensely than anyone else in the world. They seemed more like brother and sister, except perhaps that they were linking hands.

'Where have you been?' he asked.

'All over the place,' she paused. 'I met my daughters.'

'He came here,' Heath said. 'I know the score. Could you help?'

'No.' She rubbed his palm with her fingers. 'I don't want to talk about that in here. Are you clean?'

'Yes. You?'

She shook her head. 'I'm sorry.'

'That's all right, baby, that's all right. We don't have to fucking do what people tell us to do. Life's too short.'

'You have to get out.'

'And I will. I've been a good boy this year. I'm going to write the best letter this time. I've got it sussed. I'll be out in weeks. But I need an address to go to. Where are you going to stay?'

'I'll get somewhere in Glasgow. Can you get transferred in the meantime?'

'I'll get onto it. Tell me as soon as you know where we'll be living.'

'We'll be living together!' she said. 'Oh, thank God. I can't take it without you. No one else gets me.'

'No one else loves you like me,' he said. 'No one ever has. No one ever will. Cynthia, when I get out, will you marry me?'

He'd asked her this a hundred times over the years. The answer was always yes.

Somehow, they always seemed to forget to actually do it, never mind the fact that she and Will had never divorced.

'Yes!' she said. 'Of course I bloody will.'

When the visit was over, Cynthia kissed her pinky and pressed it against Heath's lips. 'I missed you.'

32

Preston felt all shaky when he walked out of the Merchant City. My Lordy, that had been quite something. He'd never seen anything like it in his life. It was as if she knew he was there. He wondered, as he began the long walk towards Charing Cross, when she'd notice what he'd taken this time. The pants she'd left on the floor of the living room when she went to take a shower. He held them in his hand and smiled.

When he got home, his mother was watching recorded snooker and chain smoking. The room smelt like pubs used to smell, before the ban.

'Hi, son,' she said. His mother had long forgotten how normal people spend their nights. Widowhood had turned everything topsy-turvy. 'Did you have a good day?'

'Yeah thanks, Mum,' Preston said, taking a plastic lunch bag from the kitchen drawer. He placed Georgie's pants in the bag and carefully sealed the plastic strip shut. 'I'm going to bed now though, okay?'

'Okay, son,' she said, leaning so he could kiss her on the cheek without getting in the way of the snooker.

Preston placed the plastic bag on top of his bedside table, took off his jeans, T-shirt, briefs and socks, and got into bed. He conjured the memory quickly, staring at the pants in the bag and touching himself. She was an extraordinary girl. Her body was immaculate considering it was screwed up inside. She moved like a swan — well, maybe not a swan. He'd never seen swans do that stuff. But it was more than her body or her face. She had an energy that zapped the space around her. She made everything stand up, as part of him was now.

It was all going to plan when the doorbell rang. He looked at the clock. 4 a.m. Who on earth? He quickly reached for his briefs and listened as his mother opened the door . . . girl rhubarb boy rhubarb boy rhubarb . . . Footsteps . . . knock, knock. 'Preston, love?'

★   ★   ★

As murders go, Preston had committed the least perfect. Each step he had taken from the Gorbals police station to the sixteenth floor of the nearby high rise, to the taxi on Rutherglen Road, had been caught on CCTV. The baseball cap had obscured his face until he took it off and threw it in the bin before getting in the taxi. Sure, the police didn't have his face on record, but in the end, they didn't need it, because the four boys he'd met outside the police station had given his name to the police — which in fact was several hours after the murder as they had been waylaid by a fight down the arches. Preston was angry with himself. He'd assumed the boys would never talk to the police, but of course they would when one of their own had been murdered. Why had he told them his real name? Preston scolded himself as he dressed. This was a most uncharacteristic security lapse.

'Preston, love?' he heard his mother say as he opened his bedroom window and climbed outside onto the ledge. He'd been doing this for years now, had it down pat.

'Preston? The police are here to . . . '

He reckoned his feet probably hit the ground just as his mother opened the bedroom door.

He reckoned police sirens started blaring just as he closed the taxi door.

33

Will held Georgie in bed until she finally cried herself to sleep. Why had he found no photographs like this — with the two of them lying on the sofa watching *Back to the Future* or *The Truman Show* or snuggling on the beach in Largs after that smile-less shot had been snapped? ('Hug me, Daddy! Hold me tighter!') Her angry adolescence seemed to have toyed with his memory, twisted everything into a negative. Sure, she was always a challenge, but she was also incredibly affectionate at times. Feisty, fiery, emotional and raw. These are the words that should have come to mind earlier.

Certain that she was sleeping calmly, Will crept out of her room, returned to his office, opened his notebook, looked at the first page:

1) Cynthia

And the second:

2) Parents

And turned to the next page to consider option number three.

3) Buy one

The knowledge of the page he had ripped out earlier throbbed in time with his hangover. Had he really been so drunk as to write such nonsense?

'How to buy a kidney.' He typed the words into the Google search engine. The very first article caught his eye:

Mother to spend life savings on kidney in Philippines

45-year-old Janette Graham, who has waited over three years for a transplant with the NHS, has decided to remortgage her house to purchase a kidney in the Philippines.

'I have grappled with the moral issues involved,' she says, 'but I have five children under the age of eighteen. I want to see them grow up.'

Mrs Graham is on dialysis every day. She fears she will die waiting for a suitable donor, as her blood type is rare and the NHS has so far failed to find a match.

Transplant tourism has become so common in the Philippines in recent years that Luzon has been nicknamed 'One Kidney Island'. 'There are people in the Philippines who see this as an opportunity to break out of debilitating poverty,' Mrs Graham says. 'I am aware of the risks involved. Some patients have not returned from their operations in South East Asia.' However, she goes on to say, she is also aware that three patients die every day waiting for a kidney transplant. 'I can't buy one here,' she says. 'It is illegal. I feel I have no other option.'

Within the article was a link to another item about Filipino donors. It was the photograph that caught Will's eye. Ten men — no, *boys* — standing in line, holding their shirts up to reveal the scars in their sides. Each had received a cash payment of £1,000, which would have provided temporary relief from poverty, but not a long-term solution. To add to that, the article highlighted that there was no evidence regarding the number of donors who had died during the procedure or from post-operative infections.

The boys in the photograph gave reasons for their decision to donate:

I haven't got a job.
My friend sold his and he was okay.
I was scared, but my brothers and sisters
needed to eat.
I wasn't scared. I was excited.

Will printed out the articles, folded them and stapled them to the back of the page in his notebook. He was torn by the risks involved and by the stark images of the boy donors, but he was also excited. The risks were less than those the girls faced at the moment. And the donors were willing, desperate even. His parents could give him the money — the fact that they had been tested indicated a willingness to help. Failing that, he could remortgage the house — enough for a kidney and enough to tide them over till everything was back to normal. He was glad not to be working right now. He had more important things to do.

The good thing about the Philippines was the sheer number of donors. One slum alone was called 'Kidney Market' because 300 people out of 16,000 had donated there. Also, the recipient made a 'donation' rather than a formal payment (around £40,000). The operations took place in a clean private hospital where the procedure was carried out efficiently and effectively. He did worry that it cost £40,000, when the donors in the photograph had only received £1,000. But with Georgie's plea fresh in his mind, he didn't wonder for long. Anyway, perhaps he could send the donor something extra (a tip, or perhaps he could deposit something each year, an ongoing thank you) to the person involved.

Will looked at several other links — a forum where potential donors had listed their wares:

Hello,
I am kairav, from INDIA 18 yrs of age, quiet healthy, have no desease and my blood group is B+. I want to sell one of my kidney.

hi
my name is anum
iam 21 years old, in good health, i have no desease, i am from egypt blood group A
87 KG

me Ekagrah. i m from india. i wanna sell 1 of my kidney as i m in need of money.

*whoever wants to buy plz contact me at
my email I WANNA SELL MY
KIDNEY*

*I want sell my kidney. 20 y.o.
Blood AB IV Rh+*

Once, Will had written something similar
for the *Glasgow Extra*.

*Double buggy for sale,
Good condition,
Can deliver*

As he continued his research, he noted that
someone had decided against a kidney from
China. The prospective patient was appalled
by the fact that it would come from an executed
prisoner. Will scoffed at this. What difference
did it make? He didn't believe kidneys had
morals which could seep into new homes. His
girls' kidneys certainly showed no moral fibre,
giving up the ghost as they had.

He felt the Philippines was the best option,
mostly because he had found more concrete
information about it than the other countries.
He wrote the necessary contact details and
the price in his notebook. He would email the
hospital later in the day. First, he had to visit
his parents in St Andrews.

34

'Georgie! Georgie! Wake up.' Kay opened the curtains of her sister's bedroom. 'It's four o'clock, G. It's a glorious day. Do you know where Dad is?'

'Shut them!' Georgie sought refuge from the light under her duvet.

'Your room is disgusting!' Kay picked up the clothes that were strewn all over the floor and piled them on a chair. She noticed a mobile amongst the debris and looked at it.

'Georgie! Your phone is off! Are you crazy?' She turned on the cheap mobile — they had both bought the same one after joining the waiting list. 'Never ever turn this off or let it run out of battery. Always keep it beside you. Are you listening?'

'Get out,' she answered. 'Stop moving my things!'

Kay ignored her sister's instructions. She put the phone on the bedside table and checked her own, which — as usual — was in her pocket. Since the diagnosis, she only ever wore clothes with pockets that would safely house her phone. She separated Georgie's dirty clothes from the clean ones and placed the former in the washing basket.

'When did they let you out?' Georgie asked.

'An hour ago. I got a taxi.'

'You're feeling better?'

'Much. Just a bit wobbly.' Kay sat on the bed and pulled the duvet down so she could see Georgie's face. 'What did you think of her?'

Georgie sighed and pulled at her fringe. 'She's . . . not what I expected.'

'Really? She's been a junkie for years, y'know. Dad said she was using when we were babies, though he didn't realise at the time. Must take its toll.'

'You think she really wanted to do the right thing?' Georgie asked.

'I reckon she knew she wouldn't be able to.'

'So now we just wait.' Georgie was really asking her sister a question. They'd never broached the subject, but they both knew the options.

'It's the only thing we can do. Isn't it?'

'No, it's not,' Georgie said. She sat up and took a sip of water from the glass beside her bed. 'You're sicker than me.'

'I'm not really. It's horrible, isn't it? Waiting for someone to die.'

'I know.'

208

'I am okay, though. I feel fine,' Kay said.

'You do not. You already look dead.'

'Thanks.'

The girls were silent for a moment, Georgie fiddling with the edge of the bed sheet nervously, Kay watching her.

'You should have his,' Georgie said, looking up. 'We should tell him to just go ahead with the test and the rest.'

'No. I absolutely refuse. If he can only help one, then it's not going to be me.'

'Well, I feel the same,' Georgie said.

'Then we wait.' Kay paused a moment. 'I'm scared, G.'

'Come here,' Georgie said, pulling her sister to her. 'Lie beside me for a bit.'

Kay lay down. 'What do you think's going to happen?'

Georgie smiled. Whenever Kay felt down about something, she always began with this sentence. Georgie had always been a star at saying the right things. Some examples:

After Kay was bulled by Felicity Kearney in Primary One (Miss Kearney put an extraordinary amount of chewed Hubba Bubba in her hair. She had to have her hair cut three inches shorter to get it all out):

What do you think's going to happen?

I think Felicity Kearney is going to get so fat she explodes.

Only a few months ago, when Graham of the trombone asked her to go out with him again or he would have to move on:

What do you think's going to happen?

I think you're going to say yes and I think you're gonna do it big time and I think it's going to be great fun.

After the blood was taken:

What do you think's going to happen?

I think whatever it says I'll be there with you every step of the way.

Now, Georgie found it as easy as ever to say the right thing:

'You know what I think, Miss K? I think the waiting will drive us mad for a while, but we'll look after each other. We'll get through it. And one day . . . when we're on the loo or eating crunchy-nut cornflakes or watching *Skins* and not even thinking about it . . . ' Georgie stroked her special phone . . . 'these little black things here are gonna go *ring ring ring!*'

35

Will arrived in North Queensferry at 10.15 a.m. His parents' routine had always been military — wake at 7, breakfast at 7.30, walk at 8.30, housework/newspapers (mother/father) at 9.30. He wondered if he should wait until his mother had finished mopping the floors (10.30) and decided not to.

'William! What a lovely surprise,' his mother said, her face contradicting her statement. She held the mop in her hand, did not want to let it go. 'Come in! Mind and don't walk on the kitchen floor. I'm halfway through.'

His father put his paper down and stood to shake his hand. 'Well well! How nice. Do you want a coffee? Margaret, can you put on some coffee?'

Will's mother quickly cleaned the rest of the floor and went over it with a special drying mop. Cleaning apparatus neatly stored, she set to with the coffee machine.

He filled them in as quickly as possible — I found Cynthia . . . She can't help us . . . Kay's deteriorating quickly . . . Waiting list is now even longer . . . 'My only option now is to purchase one from a living donor and that's why I'm here.' There, he'd blurted it out.

His mother dropped the milk. 'Oh dear,' she said. 'Now look what I've gone and done.'

The following hour felt exactly the same as when Will had told them he was doing Visual Arts . . .

. . . which was simply wrong for a clever person.

'The NHS is the best system in the world, son,' his father said. 'You should have faith. How long have you waited? It's not long, William.'

'But don't you understand we might lose one or both of them? Wouldn't you do anything to stop that happening?'

'Of course we will . . . We were tested, weren't we? We would have risked our lives.' God, these guys were exactly the same as Cynthia. They'd do anything if it involved doing nothing at all. 'We'll do everything we can to help you,' his mother said.

'Then help me now. You said you were selling the flats in Spain.'

'We're trying to do that, but no one's biting and no one's renting.' His father actually looked stressed talking about it. 'We've lost a lot of money, William. Even if we decided to, I'm not sure if we could.'

His mother came to the table with a tray of

coffees. Her lips were tightly clenched — a bad sign. She distributed the cups and sat down. 'We've read everything there is to read about the issue,' she said. This was her post-church voice. Every Sunday, after the minister had given his football-laden homily, she'd go over it at home afterwards, using these lips and this voice.

'The right way is the right way. You have to wait. Do you know how many people die in Third World countries selling their organs?'

'No, do you?'

Neither parent answered. There were no reliable statistics on this subject.

'The truth is, I find it morally repugnant,' Will's mother said. 'Those poor people — we'd be feeding on human misery. Is this really your solution? How could we live with ourselves? It's unscrupulous. It shows no respect for human life.'

'How can you say that? This is about the lives of your granddaughters.'

'It's like buying coffee from the Third World. Do you know how much the farmers are paid over in Guatemala? These people and their families are living in extreme poverty while the big companies are making a killing. It's the middle man who wins.'

Will took a sip from his cup. 'So where'd these beans come from, Mum?'

'That's enough, William,' his father said. 'You have your answer.'

★ ★ ★

Will arrived at the bank at 3 p.m. By 3.50 he was sitting with a young man of around nineteen. He was an impeccably dressed chatterbox whose enthusiasm surely meant he was fresh to the job. (Come on in and how are you today and take that chair it's the comfy one and these computers are so slow today and so I believe you would like to remortgage your house?)

'That's right'

'And what would that be for?'

'I'd like to buy a kidney from the Philippines.'

The young man gasped. 'A kidney from the Philippines? Wait on . . . Ah, it's a joke! Oh, ha-ha! You really had me going there. A kidney from the Philippines. Filipino Kidney. Like Filipina bride, but kidney. So . . . is it renovations? An extension?'

'Yes,' Will said, deciding the truth was obviously not the best way forward.

'Which one?'

'Which what?'

'Renovations or an extension?'

'Oh . . . um attic conversion.'

'Excellent. Always a good way to add value, particularly in your area. And what is the house in Newpark Road worth just now?'

'Three hundred and fifty thousand,' Will said. 'Maybe more if I fix a few things. It was four hundred a year back, but it's gone down with the economy and all that.'

'And your current mortgage?'

'A hundred and twenty thousand. I remortgaged a while back to fix the roof and rewire.'

'And your monthly outgoings?'

'Um . . . mortgage is eight hundred. Bills and car and insurance I suppose four hundred. Food and other things six hundred.'

'So, eighteen hundred a month gets you by?'

'Yes.'

'And your income?'

Will paused. How should he put this? 'I'm looking for work at the moment.'

Less than one minute later, the boy banker closed his office door politely, leaving Will to wander back to his car in despair.

* * *

Will had a few other options — moneylender, Linda, robbery — but, to be honest, his parents had hit a nerve. As he drove home from the bank he recalled the boys on One Kidney Island, holding their shirts up to show where they had been mutilated. It was morally repugnant. It was feeding on other people's misery. Could he really do that? Probably. God, who wouldn't, to save their child? Would his own parents really have ignored the option if he was going to die, when people were willing to save him, not forced, but willing?

On the other hand, his parents were right — the girls had only just started dialysis, the NHS was one of the best health care systems in the world.

Perhaps he should have faith in it.

Perhaps he should put that stupid notebook in his filing cabinet. Under S for stupid.

He should get a job. Pay the bills. Take care of the small things.

Wait.

36

From the bank, Will went straight to Linda's. He had planned to ask her for the money if his first two ideas failed. But now, he just wanted her to hit him. He'd never craved physical pain before, but now he ached for it. Would she please smash him over the head with a wooden spoon? He deserved it. And would it help him forget everything for one night? Just one night. Would pain make it possible?

Would Linda's husband still be there?

'Will! How are you?' Linda's husband Harry said when he answered the door. He was standing on two feet, so the kneeling situation must have come to an end. 'Come away in!'

The evening did not go to plan. Will ended up listening to Harry go on about his job, which made Will's employment history seem positively fascinating. As far as Will could tell, Harry cut newspaper clippings out of all the major UK newspapers and put them in files.

'So you're like a scrapbook maker?' Will said, praying now that the man would go away or that Linda would change the subject.

(Why was Linda just sitting there? Saying yes and ah and adding bits here and there as if she actually cared about her husband and his brain-dead bloody job.)

'No! Look, here's my card. I'm a Senior PR Consultant for J. M. Breweries.'

'Do you get free booze?'

'Of course.'

'Can I have some?'

Will was determined to get a moment alone with Linda. He would stay until the dick went to bed, or at least to another room. He had a strategy to make this happen.

'So, how's Archie doing with his history?' he asked Linda.

Linda never noticed the transformation in people when she spoke about her children. When anyone made the foolish error of enquiring about them, she would start at the beginning (in this case, with the particular aspect of the Reformation which interested Archie most, which was being taught very badly) . . .

And heads would nod ever so slightly . . . uh huh, uh huh.

She would end the beginning very slowly (in this case, with how she confronted said bad teacher about bad teaching methods) . . .

And shoulders would slump somewhat.

She would begin the middle animatedly (in

this case, with how — against all odds — her genius non-diseased still-at-school son had 'just gotten on with it' by sourcing extra reading material in the library and consulting students from other schools) . . .

And films of fluid would glaze eyes.

She would never get to the end.

But at least half of her audience would have left towards the middle of the non-end.

Which is what happened in this case. Harry, unable to get a word in and almost unable to move with boredom, stood, yawned, made an I'm-going-to-bed gesture — using prayer hands against a sideways head — and left the kitchen.

He was gone one second when Will said, 'I need you to hurt me.'

He thought it might work, at first, being assaulted in the garage with Harry in bed in the house. Will was looking forward to a slap or two — 'On the face, if that's okay,' he suggested as she moved her mouth back up towards his.

'You think you can make requests?' she said. *Exorcist* Linda had entered the room.

Before Will knew it, she had tied his arms to an unused roof rack using two bits of clothing line that she cut using scissors and then gnawing teeth. She then began to slap him on the dick. He really didn't like this. He

219

asked her to stop. She said no because he'd been a naughty boy. He said no I haven't. I'm a good guy, remember? She said oh no, you've been having an affair. And he said well but so has him upstairs, who — by the way — might hear it when I scream.

And she said shut up and do as you're told.

Doing as he was told meant not screaming when she bit into his scrotum. He found this very difficult.

It meant not yelling when she placed metal clamps on his nipples, which wasn't too hard, but not too pleasant either.

It meant not yelling 'Fucking let me go!' when she held his (not surprisingly not erect) penis and twisted it around like wet washing.

He didn't manage this. 'Fucking let me go!' Will yelled.

Linda responded by looking out of the garage window. (Harry must have heard. He turned on the bedroom light.) She grabbed her clothes, ran out of the garage, shut the door behind her, locked the back door, and disappeared into the house.

★ ★ ★

As hard as he tried, Will could not untie himself from the roof rack. She had secured his hands so tightly that the washing line wouldn't budge no matter how imaginatively he jiggled his arms and hands. The Jesus pose she had forced on him meant he couldn't reach his hands with his mouth. He was completely naked. And had no choice but to get out of the garage in this state.

When the girls were testing their adolescence, Will always knew exactly what they were getting up to. The terraced area was densely populated with busybodies who had nothing better to do than talk to each other about what so-and-so had done last night. For example:

I probably shouldn't pass this on, but Kay was kissing a boy on the pitch.

Would you want to know if Georgie was drinking, Will? Would you? She is, you know. Martha's dad from Second Avenue told Martha's mum and she told Belle next door here. She had a litre of cider down the park last night. Threw up right in front of the new deli.

So, as Will walked out of Linda's garage, somehow managing to open the back gate with two fingers, and entered the lane behind her house to begin the 200-metre walk home, he knew that the locals would either a) witness this first-hand or b) be told about it (perhaps even shown a photo of it) the following day.

He met one person on the way home. A dog walker whose daughter had gone to Brownies with Kay. She was a typical Brownie mum. Very organised, diligent with her children's uniforms, homework, activities and behaviour. A church elder at only forty-three. And a dog lover. She saw the naked man walking down the street, arms stretched out, attached to some kind of metal contraption, wrists tied to either end. She stared at him as he approached.

'Evening,' Will said.

'Evening,' she replied.

'Long story,' he said.

'Of course.' The woman had decided to be kind. She pretended that her dog needed a poo. With Will clambering past her, she moved into the gutter, turned her back to him as he clunked onwards, and said nothing more.

Ah, but she would have SO much to say about it in the morning.

★   ★   ★

Whenever Georgie got angry, she stormed out of the house and left the door open. As Will approached home, he realised that she had done this some time tonight. The front door was ajar at least ten inches. He'd usually panic and get angry — Had they been burgled? How much expensive heat had escaped? Did they live in a tent? — but not this time. This time he was overjoyed that Georgie was obviously out and that he could actually get inside. Will manoeuvred himself through the door and sideways into the kitchen, where he spent an hour retrieving a knife with his mouth, wedging it in the cutlery drawer, which he held firm with his hip, and slicing at the ties on his hands.

After he'd finished tending to the wounds on his penis, nipples and hands, he laughed. One thing about Linda: she certainly took his mind off things.

But the pain hadn't helped. There were no diversions from this terrible situation. Kay was asleep in bed. Georgie was nowhere to be seen. What had she done after dialysis? Where had she gone? And why had she walked out of the house without shutting the door this time?

37

How could I find true love with that lug of a boyfriend sucking the life out of me day in day out? Oh, Alfred, let me go.

Hopelessness was a familiar feeling. A few times, I'd even written melodramatic suicide notes and stapled them to my diary. Once I asked the guy who sold me dope if he knew how to get a gun. He said it was easy. That was the closest I'd come to actually doing it — i.e. not close at all. Truth is, I had always been a chicken-head. I hated pain. I didn't want to die. I really didn't. The kidney debacle made me realise that more than anything. I had stuff to do — love to find, a movie to make. Had I ever said that out loud? I wanted to do the very thing my father wanted to do at my age. I hoped I wouldn't be such a useless klutz at it. I'd even thought of a great film title, *Bit of Rough*. It'd be a sexy thriller. The good guy would win.

Preston had either stopped following me or gotten very good at it. It had been three days since he'd watched me in Reece's house and I hadn't spotted him since. What a weirdo, to enjoy being followed. What a weirdo, to analyse it the way I analysed everything, concluding in this case that being followed made me feel important. My every move was interesting to somebody. My stalker committed time and energy to the pursuit of me. He might have given up going for a run to see me buy a packet of fags at the corner shop. He might have missed his favourite E4 drama to see me brush my teeth.

I hadn't felt important my whole life. I had a good friend who almost made me feel that way, but when I dropped out of school she dropped out of my life. As much as I loved Kay, she made me feel the opposite of important. How can two identical people be so different — her so good at everything, me so shite?

As soon as dialysis was over, I decided to go home and get Preston's number from Dad's mobile. I'd ask him why he had stopped following me. Had he found someone else? Was there something I could do to make stalking me more intriguing for him?

Reece was on shift. He walked into the ward with a very professional I-don't-wear-women's-clothing kind of face. He set up my machine and he gave me the 'you're a dirty girl' look. It's okay to be dirty at the time, but afterwards it's a character flaw. Slutty, easy girl, he said with his eyes. I had to stop myself from leaning over and biting into his shoulder.

I was angry enough to bite very hard.

Not only had my mother turned out to be a transplant gone wrong — a yearning, a waiting, a perfect answer . . . and a rejection — but poor Evie had just died from exactly that.

She was all excited when I saw her two nights earlier. Her trolley whizzed right by me and my Alfred. She was convulsing with tears.

'Good luck, Evie!' I yelled.

'Way to go, Evie!' Kay yelled.

Just like the last scene in *An Officer and a Gentleman*. Saved, carried off, cheered.

I found out the following day that Evie's body had been downright rude to her new kidney. Rumours spread in her blood that an invader had entered the room. A battle was fought and won. It wasn't a victory for Evie, or for her granddaughter, who had loved Evie enough to donate.

Evie's Catherine Cookson DVDs were on the table in the corner. Maybe I'd watch one, to suffer in her honour.

Kay was making me angry too. Not by doing anything bad, but by going all fuzzy. It was as if she'd taken invisibility tablets which were slowly making her appear wobbly to the world. One day soon I'd turn around and she'd be gone altogether.

I missed Kay. The glass-half-full girl had turned glass-doesn't-even-exist. A few days after we met our mother figure, she decided against sitting her exams. 'I can't read more than a page without needing a rest,' she said. 'I'll do it next year.'

Next year. Would there even be a next year?

She'd taken to staying in bed most of the time. She didn't even turn the telly on. She just lay there and stroked her phone. Last night, I heard her talking to it (and there wasn't anyone on the line). 'Please please, go on, go on, you can do it,' she whispered. I didn't let her know I'd heard. She'd be embarrassed and I was the last person who should make her feel embarrassed for talking to a dead-as-doornails handset. I did it all the time.

★   ★   ★

Dialysis over, Kay and I got a taxi home. Misbehaving after dialysis was becoming unthinkable. I didn't even have the energy to walk to the pub. Instead, I poured myself a glass of water while Kay went up to her room.

Desperate Housewives was on. It made me think of Dad, who had left a message to say he was over at Linda's house. Good on him, I thought. If anyone needed to shag a desperate housewife it was him.

One of the wives was shooting at one of the other wives when the doorbell rang. I dragged myself to the front door and opened it.

'Hi, Kay,' the woman at the door said.

'It's Georgie,' I replied. 'The ugly one, remember?'

I was very glad to feel nauseous and exhausted.

Otherwise, my resources might have been irretrievably sucked into Planet Cynthia.

'I know I don't deserve it,' she said, leaning on the kitchen bench as I stood, arms folded, against the fridge. 'But I want to get to know you both. I want to make up for . . .'

She was having trouble finishing the sentence so I finished it for her . . . 'for being a crap mother'.

'Men assume women should be nurturers. It's a way for them to control us. We don't have to do what we're told to do.'

So she had come to teach me how to be a woman.

'I'll go get Kay,' I said. 'Do you want to put on some tea? Or is that an affront to your feminism?'

I went up to Kay's room.

'Kay! Our mother figure is here.' Although

she was asleep, she was still clutching her mobile.

'What?'

'Cynthia . . . our mother . . . I don't know what to call her. She's here. She says she wants to get to know us.'

'Is Dad back?'

'No.'

Kay stared at the ceiling for a moment, not deep in thought, but vacant. 'Tell her I'm asleep.'

'You sure?'

'I don't want anything to do with her. And make sure she's gone before Dad gets back. It's the last thing he needs.'

When I got back to the kitchen, mother figure had opened one of the bottles of red Dad bought earlier in the day and had poured herself a large glass.

'Help yourself,' I said.

'Can you not cut this shit and have a glass of wine with your mother?'

'Whatever.'

'You are *the* cliché, Georgie.' She poured a second glass of wine and handed it to me. 'Where's Kay?'

'Asleep. She needs her rest.'

'So she doesn't want to see me?'

'No, she doesn't want to see you.'

We drank the same way, me and my mother

figure. Neither of us let go of the glass, ever, and we drank small sips but very often. It wasn't long before she was opening another of Dad's bottles.

Mother figure had obviously rehearsed what she said next. It would have been beautiful, if it wasn't such a crock of self-indulgent shite.

'I want you to know why.'

'Tell me, then. Why? Why did you abandon us? Why did you never contact us? Not even one tiny phone call or letter or birthday card or email? Did you ever even think about us?'

'Every day! Georgie, every day. Let me explain this to you . . . '

She put on the kind of voice an ordinary mother might use when her child had done something bad, like stealing sweeties from a shop. She would make me understand the moral truth.

'I have always loved Heath. It's hard to convey just how much I love him, or even why. He's the other part of me, always has been. Your father — well, he was an interlude.'

'An interlude.'

'An attempt at mediocrity.'

'An attempt at mediocrity. Nice.'

'I had a career. Have you ever heard me sing?'

'I have.'

'Well, you should know then that I'm talented, Georgie. People said I was the next Stevie Nicks. I had to try, didn't I? Wouldn't it have been a waste not to try?'

Was she really asking me to make it better for her? To say, yes, I understand Mother, you are the next Stevie Nicks, whoever the hell that is?

'Don't you crave freedom? Don't you want to break down the walls they build around you? You're surrounded by them here!'

I didn't mean to nod.

'I needed the thing most people only dream of — freedom. And you know what?' she said, looking at the judgement in my eyes, 'I'm sick of being judged. I was a monster mother. I was angry and upset all the time. I slapped you both when he wasn't looking. I thought about throwing you out the window. I was depressed, suffocated. And I wasn't making him happy, or you girls.'

She emptied her glass and continued. 'I decided I had a responsibility to myself. If I couldn't be the person I wanted to be, how could I be the person you children wanted me to be? I'm not mentally ill. I'm not evil. Lots of women do this nowadays. Single fathers are common. Why do we judge that when we don't judge it the other way around?'

'Are you happy?'

'Not without Heath. I need him . . . I count the hours till I can see him.' She paused, bit her nails. 'I do understand I was awful. I let you down. I spoilt it all. I ruined it all. But I didn't think you should have to face the consequences of my behaviour.'

'You really think we didn't?'

'I think you're both outstanding people. That's what I think. If I'd stayed, I'm not so sure.'

There, she'd finished her speech. She sighed with self-satisfaction. 'Where's Will?' she asked, her tone different now.

How dare she call him Will? I thought. 'At his girlfriend's.' I loved saying that. Was she jealous? Did she feel anything in those huge blue eyes? Not as far as I could tell. Although she was a little sweaty. Had an itch on her chest she couldn't relieve.

'He's a good man. I knew he'd be a good father to you.'

I felt like telling her the truth: that he was a lazy no-hoper who'd wasted his life and done nothing. Instead, I said, 'He is good. You did the right thing.'

'Can I look at some photos?' she asked. 'I want to see you as little girls.'

I looked in the glass-fronted cabinet, but most of the albums weren't there. 'I'll check in the office,' I said, making my way into Dad's private room off the lounge.

The room was always messy, but blimey, what had he been doing in there? Books and notebooks and photo albums and report cards and glasses and empty bottles of wine were strewn all over the floor. The filing cabinet was open. The drawer to his desk was so full of crap that it hadn't closed properly, and — Ha! I knew it! — several joint stubs were on the top of the filing cabinet in a wee saucer. Sneaky wee bastard. I grabbed the photo albums and went back into the living room.

I hate to admit it, but I was really excited at the idea of sitting with her on the sofa, showing her what we looked like as kids, telling her the things we'd been doing in the photographs.

'We were so cold that day!' I was going to say, for example, when I showed her the photograph at Loudoun Castle. 'The three of us had a picnic on the grass and had to practically sit on top of each other to keep warm. Dad's a good cuddler. So's Kay.'

I didn't say this, because my mother figure, God bless her cotton socks, said, 'I've signed on today. They've put me in some hostel till I get my own flat.'

'That's good.' I pointed at the Loudoun Castle photo, still ready to impress her with emotional stories that might make her cry.

'Thing is, it takes a while,' she said.

'This is at Loudoun Castle,' I said.

'Around two weeks, for the money to come through.'

My face went hot all of a sudden. 'You want money?'

'I can't believe I'm asking you this. I feel ashamed, Georgie.' She actually took the album out of my hand, closed it, and put it on the coffee table. 'I am a heroin addict . . .' She paused for dramatic effect. 'There, I've said it.'

My turn to pause, not for dramatic effect, but because my jaw refused to return to its rightful place. Eventually it did, and I said, 'Go to your GP. Get on methadone.'

'I was struck off a while before I left. I've requested another one. Again, it can take a while. Plus, I have to stay clean long enough before they consider me for meth, prove I'm susceptible to treatment. It's a catch 22. I just need enough to tide me over.'

Oh, the itch. She was going at it like mad now.

'So you came here because you want me to give you money for heroin.'

'No, no, no, no!' she said, reading the anger in my voice and regretting her honesty. She picked up the album with shaky hands and opened it again. 'Tell me about this photo. Is it in England?'

She was biting her hand — not her nails, but the actual flesh on her hand. And rocking back and forth a little.

'It's in Loudoun Castle,' I said. 'It was cold that day. Dad is a good cuddler.'

'Cold, hey?' she said, her eyes flickering from one side of the room to the other.

There were two things going on in my head. The first was that I didn't like anything about my mother. There was nothing to like. She was a drugs sponge, that was all, nothing more.

The second was that I didn't want to give her money for drugs. 'I'll give you food,' I said, slamming the album shut and putting it out of reach on the floor by my side of the couch.

'I'm not hungry!' she said. 'Okay, it is for drugs. But can't you understand? Haven't you ever needed something so badly you could explode?'

'Let me think.' She didn't note the sarcasm. Did she even remember why my father had sought her out?

She didn't start crying, but I think she

wanted to — it would have helped with the performance. Instead she grabbed my hand and scrunched her face into a crying face and said, 'Please, Georgie. Even just twenty quid. Come on! I'd do it for you.'

'If I agree, do you promise to get a drugs counsellor or something?'

'I promise! I'll go to that place down the Gorbals. You don't even need to make an appointment.' She'd let go of my hand. Scrunched-up-crying-face suddenly became excited-'cause-I'll-be-off-my-head-soon face.

I pulled my hands from hers and got my purse from the hall table. There was nothing in it. No surprise, really, as no one in our house had an income. Pocket money had stopped along with the rentals in Spain. But Dad always kept emergency money in the filing cabinet under E. Retard. I went back into his office and opened the cabinet.

Was that my diary on his desk? What the fudge! Putting that issue to the side for a moment, I retrieved a twenty-pound note from a small leather wallet in the filing cabinet, shut it, and handed it to my mother figure, who was now drooling at the door of the office.

'So, you have got somewhere to stay?'

'Aye. This hostel in Govanhill for now, but I'll get a furnished flat from the council soon as the benefits are sorted.'

'Let me know when you're settled.'

'Thank you, Georgie. I mean it. Thank you.'

There were no kisses or hugs. I closed the door and sighed.

★ ★ ★

What was my diary doing in Dad's office? I went back in and lifted it from his desk. Had he read it? He better bloody not have. Kay's was underneath it. What was he doing with our diaries? Both had been placed on top of a brown notebook. Without thinking, I opened the notebook and read the first line of the first page.

1) Cynthia

Typical Dad. Years ago, when he announced that he was going to make another attempt at a screenplay, he locked himself away in the office for weeks, finally appearing, triumphant, with a similar notebook. In it, he had made a very long list indicating how he was going to write the thing.

1. Treatment

2. Synopsis

3. Tagline
*4. Approach Scottish Screen with all of
the above with view to getting script
development money.*
5. Write two scenes per day.
*6. Research which producers are hot at
the moment.*
7. Meet them! Network!

The plan had seventy-five points, each with
around five sub-points. He read it to us in the
living room, proud of himself for making it.
Dickhead.

'You should just write it,' I remember
saying when he'd finished reading.

He went back to his office in a huff,
puncturing the list onto the metal spike he
put all his defunct lists on. It was half full of
lists, this spike. Dead lists.

So this was his plan now — to write useless
notes about how he might save us.

Cynthia. Okay, so — unusually — he had
actually found her, but it hadn't helped. What
was next on his list of things to either not do
or do badly?

Parents — useless pricks.

Buy one.

Oh my God, he'd printed out a picture of
boys with scars, standing in line in their slums
in the Philippines. How could he even think

of this? It made me feel sick. Did he really believe we would agree to the idea? Even if it saved our lives? Well, okay, maybe. Probably.

His notes about how to raise the forty grand made me laugh. His parents! The stingy stuck-up pricks that they were.

The bank! What did he think they'd say? 'Yes, here you go — O unemployed single parent — off and join the black-market organ trade.'

The next way to raise the cash was 'Linda'. That must be why he went there tonight. Should I go over there and tell him to stop this nonsense? That I hated the idea of paying for a body part from some poor child? I felt sure that Kay would feel the same. Yes, I decided I should go over there and confront him about it.

But what was that — a blank page in the notebook followed by a missing one. He must have ripped one out. Why? I looked in the bin. It wasn't there. Checked on the desk and floor — nup. Opened the drawer of his desk . . . Ah, look, there it was. A ripped, scrunched page. I sat down, straightened it out, pieced it together, and contemplated the headings: GEORGIE and KAY; PROS and CONS.

38

I was born unhappy and I stayed that way.
I have found it difficult to conform.
I am mean.
Selfish.
Horrible.
I have no hope.
No ambition.
No kindness.
I love no one bar a junkie who does not love
me, she loves my twenty quid.
I hate my father.
He hates me too.
I never knew.
Till now.
Do I want to kill him?
It's very easy to get a gun.
I hate everything.
I want to die.

Thanks Dad, for writing the perfect note. He had a thing about notes, ever since she left, without leaving so much as a scribble. And this was a masterpiece: the screenplay he never started let alone finished.

Oh shut up Georgie and find that bottle.

You should cry Georgie, you should.

Ah, there it was, in the bag, along with what? Cigarettes.

The station.

Trains leave for Central at nine minutes past the hour.

Did Kay call my name as I left? I wasn't sure. My ears had stopped hearing. Did it matter that I was barefoot? In just jeans and a T-shirt at ten to nine on a weekday?

My feet had stopped feeling.

One step then another and another. The train would come soon and I didn't want to miss it. It was a further grand thing about our suburb, the train line, leaving at nine minutes past the hour every hour. The train line and the schools.

I didn't care when young girls stared on the way back from Brownies.

Oh, that was another thing about our area, Brownies.

I didn't care when a woman stared from her front door, waiting for the Tesco delivery man to empty the van and fill her kitchen.

A car may have tooted as I crossed the road to the station. May have even screeched a little. I had my bottle in my hand now. The walking was necessary. Nothing could stop me.

I am mean.

Am I mean?

There were boys on the ramp, smoking boys. I walked past them, down to the platform. It was one minute past nine. A middle-aged man sat on the bench reading the business section of his paper. He was going out of town. Must have gone to the pub round the corner on the way back from work. Probably had a job in the city and went to important meetings that required dark grey suits and a knowledge of the business section of the *Herald*. When his train came, he would head further into suburban wilderness where there are no pubs.

I didn't want him to see me. I walked to the other side of the platform, sat on the edge, and drank a quarter of my bottle.

I am selfish.

Am I selfish?

I suppose there is evidence. If Dad buys Doritos and I find them first, I eat them all.

The smoking boys on the ramp were laughing at me. Once I might have cared but I didn't care about anyone any more.

Ah, I am all of the above.

The train came and went on the other platform, along with the businessman.

It was five minutes past nine.

I want to kill my father.

Do I want to kill my dad?

I wonder if he wrote it quickly, discovered it quickly, or did he agonise over it like the screenplay he never wrote a few years back?

I have found it hard to conform.

Have I?

I drank another quarter of my bottle.

I want to die.

Do I?

Four minutes until my train, my end, would arrive. Before that, two questions. I felt anxious to answer them in time.

Do I have nothing to live for?

What will it feel like, dying this way compared to slowly merging with my Alfred?

I supposed it would feel scary for a moment, then very sore, sorer than anything you could imagine, then maybe you might hear something, a screeching of brakes, perhaps, or the smoking boys on the ramp screaming — no, yelling, because they're boys. Or maybe the silence would arrive sooner, even sooner than the soreness. So really all you'd have is the scary part, and I was already fucking scared so another scary thing, big scary train, wouldn't bother me. No, I concluded, this could be a good way to die compared to merging with my Alfred.

Georgie and Alfred: *They lived together. They died together. It was hard to tell them* apart towards the end. *Whose tube was that? Whose was that red stuff? Who was that sniggering?*

But, hey, I'd only answered the easy question.

The first was the hardest. *Do I have nothing to live for?* 'Let me think,' I said out loud. 'What do people normally have to live for?'

If it's happiness, I'm fucked.

If it's money, I'm fucked.

If it's procreation, I'm fucked.

If it's hope . . .

If it's loving . . .

Oh, okay, I see.

Something pinged, made me look around. The screen on the platform was flashing with a fresh message. THE 9.09 TO GLASGOW CENTRAL HAS BEEN CANCELLED DUE TO AN EVENT IN NEILSTON. ALL TRAINS CANCELLED UNTIL FURTHER NOTICE.

Ha! The train was cancelled. I didn't believe in messages from God, didn't even believe in God, but the train was cancelled!

* * *

I have an incredible *staracity*, a word I made up to define my skill for doing what I do for hours each day. Stare. At bloody nothing. For ages.

I was walking along the train tracks. What had happened in Neilston to cancel my train? An *event*. Big word, event. Either a meteor had struck it or there'd been a jumper. Something death-related, anyway. When I died, would my father tell people he'd had an event? 'I'm so sorry to hear about your event,' they might write on white cards embossed with smug silver barely coating the secret message: 'Thank God it's you who had the event. We have not had one. Go, us!'

In the Neilston case I supposed someone down the road had asked himself: *What do people normally live for?* and he had worse answers than me. I had scored one and a half out of five — some hope, a strong desire for loving. He might have got one, or none, which meant he had no choice but to jump — or gently lower himself down and stand — in front of the train that was obviously not destined for me. I passed the test. Well, that was something.

I was walking along the train tracks. I had consumed one whole bottle of vodka. My feet were bare. I wanted to find the right place to stare. I was looking forward to it. People who don't have good staracity don't know what they're missing. When I stare, I turn what's in front of me into something altogether different. Not better, necessarily. Sometimes much worse. But that can be an excellent thing, returning to reality and finding it's an improvement on the mass murder in your stare, that everything in the real world is actually less bloody. It's the best thing to do at times like these.

Had there ever been times like these? Had someone else found the mother she craved more than her mother craved heroin — only to be sliced open to no avail? Had anyone else been hit twice by Will Marion, who slaps faces fucking hard and who loves my sister more than he loves me?

He was going to let me go.

He was going to save Kay.

He was going to let me go.

He'd never made one decision, my father, not one, in his whole life, and this is the one.

★   ★   ★

I reached the perfect place, up the platform, over the bridge; the skateboard park. Large and green, this park. Ominous, maybe even without the knowledge that a woman had been killed here not so long ago, dragged from the sidewalk and inside to be raped and strangled and turned into posters and yellow plastic police strips. Sitting on the half pipe, I wondered if being raped and strangled would be worse than my situation in any case?

Dad. I loved you, mostly. Like a scab to pick at, eat even, if no one's watching. Scabs are nice. I like a lot about them. But I despise them too. War scars. I fell off that chute. I couldn't ride that bike.

I despised you for the wrong reason. It wasn't your fault she left. It wasn't your fault and I blamed you for it. I wish now it was the right reason. Such a nice simple reason — you made her go. You never stopped her. Now I yearn for that anger. Where is anger when I need it?

Where are tears when I need them?

What has happened to my staracity?

I'm supposed to go to dialysis again tomorrow.

Fuck you, Dad.

Fuck you, Alfred.

I'm not going.

39

If Kay wasn't sleeping she was flicking from one news channel to another. Afghanistan, flick. Cocaine-taking politician, flick. Pile up on the M8. STOP. Watching the footage of the M8, she'd ask herself, as she touched her phone, if this might be her kidney.

How old is the person? she'd say to the television, and if the reporter didn't answer, she'd switch to another channel to see if more information was available. If there was none, she'd say a little prayer that went like this:

Please, oh please God, let that be mine.

She felt bad that she didn't say 'or Georgie's'.

For the last few days she'd flicked through her waking hours — news, news and the occasional ad that interested her:

'Three people die every day waiting for a kidney . . . Please register as a donor now.'

Please register now, she'd say. *I am the weak dying guy in the chair on that ad. I'm waiting for the flesh that you won't need.*

Apart from the ad, it was the news.

There was a drowning in the Clyde. Could be hers.

A murder in Pollok. Would that one do?

A fire in Edinburgh. Too damaged?

The morning after Georgie ran off — ignoring her plea to 'Stay, don't go, I think I'm going crazy!' (Did Georgie even hear? It was unlike her to leave her sister in distress) — Kay turned on the news, got out of bed, showered, dressed, and walked to the train station. There'd been a death at Neilston. A man of twenty-four had jumped in front of the train to Glasgow Central. His name was John Bain. *John Bain*, she asked herself as she walked towards the station, *have you got my kidney?*

She knew it was silly before she arrived at Neilston. The body would be well gone. Everything would be back to normal. But she couldn't help herself. She needed to see first hand the kind of incident that she longed for.

The body was gone. The trains were running on schedule. John Bain had either been too squished, donated to someone else or had failed to register as a donor.

Kay didn't want to go home. Like looking very hard in the direction a bus was supposed to come from — any time soon, any time soon, relax your neck and you'll miss it — she felt she should crook her neck for her kidney.

She went into town, wandered around until she found a hospital and followed signs to the

249

Accident and Emergency Department. The waiting area was typically depressing. Plastic chairs were filled with the coughing, the bleeding, the moaning, the head-holding, the almost-puking, the drunk and the drug-addled. Pale children played with broken bits of sticky toys. Paramedics wheeled trolleys through double doors. Receptionists noted walking wounded details through thick glass:

'Mrs Malloy . . . chest pains, you say? Go to room 5!'

'Mr Thomas . . . when did the rash appear? Where is it? On the groin area? Take a seat.'

'Miss Carroll . . . ring stuck on your finger? We'll call your name.'

'Mr King . . . you're looking unsteady. Car accident? Mr King? Mr King? Nurse!'

And so on.

Kay watched intently. The man leaning over the cardboard puke container — was he dying? Should I ask him? The teenager lying unconscious on the trolley in the corridor. Could I have hers? The middle-aged woman with chest pains being taken in for a scan. Ask her, ask her, before the second attack. Have you registered? Would you please consider me?

If she waited long enough, Kay thought, maybe hers would arrive.

40

Will woke late and sore. Even his penis was bruised. Out of the bedroom (or garage), Linda was a sweet person, a close friend, called him 'Good Guy', made muffins. Inside, she was a sadistic nutjob wringing juice from body parts with bare hands.

The house was empty. Will was glad because he had things he needed to do, privately. He went into his office before his morning coffee, picked up his notebook (had he left it open?) and sat on the sofa bed. He inhaled deeply and blew the air onto the notebook. '4)' he wrote at the top of page four. He couldn't write the word. How could he? Then, if he couldn't write it on a piece of paper, how would he ever do it?

'Suicide.'

Will felt he'd already done it. Like scratching 'I love Cynthia' on the fence of the Bothy after their third date all those years ago. If he hadn't loved her before that scribe, he felt he must after.

About 55,600,000 search results. Suicide was a popular subject. He narrowed the criteria: 'How to commit suicide safely', deleted 'safely', as it was ridiculous, and clicked on Wikipedia's succinct guide to the choices available.

Options now forming a list in his notebook, Will pondered, scoring them out of ten thus:

1. Pesticides
Would screw up organs.
0/10

2. Bleeding/wrist cutting
I'm too scared. And apparently this can be much worse than you expect.
2/10

3. Drowning
How would they get me out of the loch/river/swimming pool? Timing would be very difficult. Would need a fit attendant. 1/10

4. Suffocation
Hard to manage head bag on my own. Would naturally fight against it.
2/10

5. Electrocution
Ow! Can get seriously burnt too. Still . . . prettyquick.
4/10

6. Jumping
Afraid of heights and kidney may be pulp.
0/10

7. Firearms
Hmm.
8/10

8. Hanging
Oh but do I have to? If you get it wrong, it can go on for ages. If you get it right . . .
7/10

9. Vehicular impact — Rail/subway train
See '6. Jumping' above.
0/10

10. Poisoning — Pesticide poisoning/Drug overdosing/Carbon monoxide poisoning/Other toxins
Would probably damage organs. Not 100% sure how much.
3/10

11. Immolation
Death by fire, methinks not.
0/10

12. Seppuku
Samurai warrior style. Could I be a warrior? Maybe.
Could I dress up all fancy?

12a. Research dress requirements and purchase online
Could I hold my sword before me?

12b. Buy sword
Could I place my special cloth beneath?

12c. Need special cloth as well
Could I read my death poem?

Often sidetracked, Will set to on the death poem required for a Samurai warrior to commit seppuku. One hour and seventeen scrunched sheets of A4 printing paper later, this was the result:

12d. Death Poem
I've always found it difficult
To choose the perfect gift
Till now.
Smile about this.
Please, when you open this,
Smile.
Though wrapped with love,
The paper is meaningless

254

As I've only ever lived through you
And this way
I can continue.

He was pleased with the poem. It made him cry. He wiped his tears and wrote:

Could I open my kimono, take up my short sword and plunge it into my abdomen?
Could I make a cut to the left, a cut to the right, an upwards stroke?
I would need an attendant.

12e. Find attendant who does not think this all too weird
The attendant, standing by on the second stroke, would perform daki-kubi when I was all but decapitated, leaving a slight band of flesh attaching my head to my body.
Fuck it, that sounds dreadful.
0/10

13. Apocarteresis (suicide by starvation)
Very slow. And I've never been able to resist crisps.
If someone offers me one, I'll just eat it.
0/10

14. *Explosion*
Ha! NO!
0/10

15. *Suicide attack (like a suicide bomber)*
No need to kill anyone else.
0/10

16. *Indirect suicide (get a cop to shoot me . . . i.e.*
force someone else into doing it)
Have to take someone hostage or something. Too hard. Might shoot my kidneys.
0/10

17. *Assisted suicide . . .*

Okay, here we go! Legal, painless. Just need compelling reason to die. (What could be more compelling than my reason?) Dignified, not scary, kind, clean, calm.

★ ★ ★

As he googled, he became more and more excited. Dignitas! People went there all the time. Never came back, mind.
Dignitas, the Swiss suicide clinic, the

256

five-star suicide clinic, the suicide clinic voted by users as the best suicide clinic in the world. Could it be painless? Could he arrange safe, immediate transplants in Switzerland?

He'd considered being a kidney tourist, why not a suicide tourist? He'd always wanted to travel.

He read everything there was to read about it online. It was a crushing blow when he discovered that he needed recommendations from doctors (15g), which he would never get, and also that the girls may be prosecuted for helping him (15h).

'2/10' he wrote, downhearted.

So, he thought, perusing the very tidy list which had in fact taken up three pages after the one he'd ripped out earlier . . .

It'd have to be the gun.

41

Will opened his daughter's diary. What had she said exactly? *You'd be surprised how easy it is to get a gun.*

If *she* could find one, surely he could? Where would she have looked?

He googled, as usual, and only found one helpful article. It was titled 'Dial a gun'. Apparently it was possible to get a gun within two hours in Scotland. Unfortunately, the newspaper article did not offer the telephone number. What it did say was that gang members in Glasgow were arming themselves with guns more and more often.

What gangs did Georgie know of?

The Young Mayfield Posse, perhaps? Or The Broady up the road, regularly accused of setting fires to wheelie bins and throwing bricks into the windows of the dining rooms bordering the park?

He decided on the latter. Georgie often disappeared down to the park, often came back smelling of drink. It was dark. The local hoodlums might just be there.

The local park offered dog walking for the older residents of Will's neighbourhood and a drinking and fighting playground for their children and for the youngsters who lived on the other side of the river. They didn't have to swim over, the poor people from yonder schemes, but they had to walk further, and it was worth it, because in the park there was always something going on.

Like tonight.

A group of ten or so boys aged around seventeen were hanging around the lane that separated the park from the terraces. Swearing loudly and throwing bottles at the bench, they noticed him coming and quietened slightly. Maybe he was a cop, they probably thought. Or just some middle-class arsehole come to make their lives more interesting.

'Excuse me!' Will said before he got too close. 'I want to talk to the leader.'

The boys laughed. Like they had a leader. Like they weren't fuckin' democratic.

'We're socialists,' a boy yelled. 'You can talk to all of us.'

Will moved a little closer, worried a bottle might come his way, or a knife, or a bullet. 'I don't want any trouble,' he said. 'Honestly, I just need some information. I'd rather not talk to everyone.'

One of the boys stepped forward. 'Information is expensive.'

'I'll talk to you,' Will said, flashing the ten-pound note he held between his fingers to indicate that, yes, the boy would be paid for his cooperation.

They spoke in the bushes halfway down to the river. 'I need a gun,' Will said. 'Just feeling tetchy, would like to have one in case of trouble, you know?'

The young man burst out laughing. 'A gun? You kidding me? Why would I know how to get a fucking gun?'

'Sorry,' Will said. 'I just thought . . . '

'I know exactly what you thought, you stuck-up prick. Now fuck off,' he said, taking the ten pounds.

* * *

Hmm. Okay, that didn't go to plan. Will decided to try another tack. He went home, got his car keys and drove to the roughest pub in town. It was in the East End, a notorious haunt for Glasgow gangsters. Cynthia used to meet Heath there for a drink. ('He's an old friend, Will. I need to keep up with my friends!' she used to say.)

The pub looked like an oversized shipping container rendered in grey concrete. Will was scared as he walked in, although no one turned around, no one stopped talking. They liked strangers in these parts.

'Pint, thanks,' he said as calmly as he could, downing it quickly with a trembling hand and ordering another.

A group of middle-aged men spoke seriously in the corner. Looked like the guys in *The Sopranos*, only weedier and scarred and pinched. He waited till one of them went to the loo, and followed him in.

It probably wasn't gangland etiquette to do business while pissing. Nevertheless, Will decided to broach the subject full flow. 'You know who I should speak to here?' he said, pleased with how cryptic he was being.

'Anyone you like,' the guy said, not flinching, shaking his dick, zipping his fly, and leaving.

He returned to the bar, ordered another pint, and when he felt drunk enough, he said to the barmaid, a woman of around fifty, with bleached hair and orange make-up, 'You know where I can get a gun?'

The barmaid looked at him like he was an alien. 'No,' she said, moving to the other end to take an order.

Shit, this was not going well. It wasn't easy to get a gun at all. He sipped his beer slowly, his mind racing as to the next option — Gun shop? Rifle club? — when a man in his thirties, with a scar from right ear to lip, sat beside him, whisky in hand, and said, 'What type you looking for?'

Surprised at the sly and excellent exchange of information in the establishment, Will said, 'Handgun. And bullets. Long as it works, if you know what I mean. I have cash.'

'Sorry,' the guy said. 'Can't help you.'

Will watched the man leave the bar and walk over to his table. He sighed, downed the rest of his drink and stood to leave. As he did, he noticed a beer mat in front of him, which had a phone number written on it in blue ink.

In the car outside the pub, Will dialled the number. 'Hello?' he said. 'I was talking to someone in the pub just now.'

'Alexandra Park, just inside the entrance, one hour,' a male voice said.

The man in the park wasn't the one he'd met at the bar. This one was barely twenty, wearing jeans and a hoody. He had a suitcase in his hand. 'Two hundred,' was all he said.

Will counted the moncy, handed it over and took the suitcase, not knowing what was inside, hoping, praying, that it would be the gun he had ordered, forgetting that what he'd ordered was the weapon he would use to take his own life.

★ ★ ★

At home an hour later, Will held the gun in his hand. He didn't know what it was called. He didn't know how to load it or use it, or anything. It was icy cold, small, scary. He touched it tentatively, put it on his desk, and wrote under section 7:

7a. Work out how to use it

He searched a long time before the correct image appeared on screen and took his time practising how to load and where to squeeze. Satisfied he had this right, he turned to:

7b. Where to shoot

In the head, he decided. Right temple.

7c. Where to do it

He had to be reasonably close to a hospital, or at least he needed to know that an ambulance was on its way. He looked up the average response time for an ambulance in the area — which was twenty-two minutes. Should be fine, as long as he called first. He added:

7d. Be at home; ring ambulance first

7e. Write note to ensure kidneys are donated to the girls

As soon as the girls became ill, he'd registered as a donor, but he needed to make sure his kidneys went to the right people. He drafted the note he would write:

Dear Sir/Madam,

Please donate my kidneys to my daughters, Georgie and Kay Marion.
Yours faithfully,
Will Marion.

7f. Ring the girls and let them know they need to go to the hospital

7g. Shoot yourself in the head (right temple).

The last two points were where Will became unstuck. His handwriting became very wobbly as he wrote them down. How could he press the trigger? He imagined pressing it, holding it against his temple and just doing it. Or just not doing it.

And what would he say when he rang the girls? 'Hey, Georgie! Hey, Kay! Just ringing to say I'm about to shoot myself in the head.

Can you come home now? If you hurry, maybe you can catch a lift to the hospital with my dead body?'

They would be devastated. They would be angry. They would hate him. They would hate themselves. And go mad with the guilt.

★ ★ ★

Will hid the gun in his filing cabinet under G, closed his notebook and exploded. Tears spurted from his eyes. Liquid from his mouth and nose. His fists bashed walls. His mouth spurted words: 'I can't do it! I'm too scared! I'm a useless arsehole!'

He threw CDs from the shelf, found the one he was looking for and stamped on it. Twisted it. Stamped again. 'It's not time to say goodbye.' He fell to the ground, paused . . . 'But my list is all done. It's all done.'

Twenty minutes or so later, and a little calmer, Will lay on the carpet and hugged himself. Suicide wasn't just impossible because of his cowardice and fear, the aftermath would be unbearable for the girls. How could he leave Georgie and Kay to deal with it? Could he really do this? Would they cope?

Kay, maybe.

But Georgie? The guilt would eat her up.

She was like an emotional satellite dish, picking up signals from all around her, buzzing with worries, constantly empathising.

'What will I do?' he said out loud. 'What am I going to do?'

It took him a long time to realise that all he could do was get himself together, make sure the girls were okay and be a father to them. They were okay, weren't they?

Were they?

Where were they?

He'd been considering suicide for hours. A new day had come and gone. It was getting dark again. And the girls weren't in the house. Will phoned their personal mobiles — no answer. Most parents would ring friends or boyfriends at this point, but Will immediately rang the hospital.

'Mr Marion,' the nurse said. 'I was about to call you. Georgie and Kay didn't come in for dialysis this evening. Is everything okay?'

42

He thought I was staring but I wasn't. I could see him, standing behind the bushes, watching me. I hadn't moved for about a half an hour. Still, he watched. I'd decided that in a minute's time — I'd been counting down for twenty minutes — I was going to suddenly stand up. I wondered what he would do. How he would react.

It was time.

I stood up.

I planned to stand still for several minutes. Would he move at all? Not yet.

Several minutes later, I stretched my arms to the sky. Would he find this interesting? He hadn't moved. He was still watching. Must have found it very interesting.

I decided to walk slowly out of the park. Would he find this fascinating?

He followed me — about fifty paces behind, I reckoned — must've found it very fascinating.

I decided to run. All the way from Pollokshaws Road to Newlands Park, as fast as I could, which wasn't very fast considering my poor health and smoke-addled lungs.

He ran too, twenty strides behind. Must've been enthralled.

I decided to stare in Newlands Park. I sat by the small pond at the dip of the hill, cross-legged, and stared. I decided I would do this for two hours.

Would Preston have the stamina?

The minutes passed more quickly than I expected. In my stare, I didn't imagine so much as remember. Not bad things, to my surprise. Good things, when things were better. I remembered me and Kay as toddlers, playing on the trampoline. She had so many rules about safety, Kay. I ignored them all. Double bounced her, for example. We always ended up laughing, despite the injuries. I remembered the first grownup movie I watched with Dad. It was *Back to the Future*. We sat on the edge of the sofa the whole way through, both loving it. I remembered those stupid caravan holidays on Arran — exploring caves, climbing hills, eating too much at the pub, playing charades, the three of us snuggling in bed. I remembered Dad saying, 'I am the luckiest man alive to have you girls. I am the happiest, luckiest man alive.'

I remembered that he said this all the time, once a week or more, probably.

Each minute was filled with happy memories.

Occasionally, there were gentle interruptions from the present: a tummy rumble, a baby-filled pram stopping by the pond, a dog pooing on the grass, Preston shuffling from his chosen position behind the tennis shed, schoolchildren having a swing before homework, tea and bath, a couple, holding hands.

And then — in the second hour — this:

'Preston MacMillan, you are under arrest. Put your hands in the air.'

I saw him run from the tennis shed towards the park exit. He was a fast runner.

'Stop now!' a police officer shouted, but Preston kept running, through the park gate, across the road and up the street. I ran towards the exit to see what was happening. Three officers were chasing him on foot up the street, one of them gaining on him as he neared the main road at the end, another shouting at him to stop, another radioing for back-up. Just before the intersection, the fastest officer caught up with him and pounced on him. Panting as I reached the scene, I watched as the second officer handcuffed him and as the third radioed to cancel the back-up.

'What have you done?' I said as he lay face down on the asphalt.

As the police man-handled him across the road and into the car, Preston told me as much as he could about what happened with the drug dealer. 'Will you visit me?' he asked as they pushed him down into the back seat.

I said I would.

43

It didn't take Will long to find Kay. She was in the third hospital he called. When he arrived, she was lying across several chairs in the Accident and Emergency Department, knuckles white as she clutched her black phone in her sleep. Was that really Kay? Where had her face gone? The one with expression and colour? And her body? Once strong and vibrant, now a shell.

'Kay, honey?' Will said, touching her bony shoulder. 'Are you all right?'

She opened her eyes. 'Dad?'

'Are you all right, darlin'?'

A beat. 'I'm not. I'm really not.'

He held her as she cried. Tough, positive, non-crier Kay, sobbing in her dad's arms.

'Do you know where your sister is?' Will asked.

'No. Our mother visited Georgie last night and she ran off not long after. Didn't come back.'

'Let's go find her, darling.'

★ ★ ★

271

Will and Kay were both in a panic about Georgie when they arrived at the house, but there was no need to worry. She was there, on the sofa, staring.

She didn't talk at all as Will drove them to the hospital for dialysis. And she stared into space, comatose, while the machine went to work on her. Will sat in a chair opposite his daughters, watching blood moving through tubes, arms lumpy and throbbing at entry point. They were thin yet puffy, both of them. And yellow. And so unhappy-looking that he would have shot himself right there if the gun hadn't been filed under G in his office filing cabinet.

This room, the dialysis unit, had become their second home, and Will hated it. He hated seeing his girls tied to their machines, itching for time to pass, four long hours a shot. He hated watching the others come and go. He hated seeing the girls make friends with those whose only common features were illness, depression and this parallel world. Hated seeing them envy the ones who got the call, pity the ones who never would, hated that they both, now, seemed to have lost the will to live. The waiting, the machines, the sickness, it had driven them both mad.

When they got home five hours later, Will

stopped Georgie from following her sister upstairs. 'Can we talk?'

'Okay,' Georgie got herself a glass of water and sat down at the kitchen table. 'Let's talk about the pros and cons of Georgie Marion. There are more cons, it seems.'

Shit. Will slumped into his chair. 'Let me explain.'

'Go ahead.'

He paused. How could he explain? 'I was pissed and stoned,' he said.

'Good one. Just like Mum.'

'More than that. I was angry with you.'

'Uh-huh.'

'You make me so angry sometimes, Georgie.'

'Kill me, then. Save Kay.'

'You know why you make me angry? I realised it after I wrote it down.'

'Let me think. I'm horrible and mean and unhappy and selfish . . . what else was there?'

'Because you're right.'

'You should've listed that as a pro. Whatever that means.'

'You're right. I'm a useless arsehole. I never do anything. I never achieve anything. Can't even decide where to go abroad, so we never do.'

'So what? You want me to feel sorry for you? Help you?'

273

'No, I want you to know I love you so much. Maybe it'll make you squirm to say this, but you're my best friend in the world. I love you and Kay the same. But you *know* me. You challenge me. Every day I spend with you is a day I learn something about myself. Usually things I don't like, but you're right to show me those things.'

Georgie hadn't looked at him yet, but she was softening, he could tell.

'When your mother left you took on all the anger. Someone had to. I couldn't. I had to try and look after you. Not only that, you looked after your sister. She's actually much more vulnerable than you. More straight-forward, less moody, but I can see you in ten years' time, doing great things, Georgie, being someone really amazing . . . and being my pal. God, do you press my buttons, though.'

'You are an arsehole.'

'I know I am. A big smelly one.'

'A huge smelly one.'

'I would never choose between you. I would never ever hurt you.'

Georgie paused. 'Kay needs it most. You should force her, just tell her and that's that.'

'I can't do that. I won't. And she wouldn't

let me. Will you forgive me for what I did?'

'Yeah, I will.'

'Will you promise never to hurt yourself?'

'If you promise never to read my diary.'

As they hugged, Will whispered to Georgie, 'You remember how we used to decide where to go on holiday?'

'Bessie up or down.'

'Go get your sister.'

★ ★ ★

Will, Georgie and Kay sat around the kitchen table. Will's hands rested side by side, palms down, in the middle. Underneath was a five-pound note.

They were all staring at the hand.

'Bessie up or down?' Will asked Kay.

'Get her to choose,' she said.

Okay then, Georgie, 'Bessie up or down?'

Georgie breathed in, held her chin up with her fists, breathed out, stared at her father's hands, and said . . . 'UP.'

Kay bit at the inner lining of her lip. Georgie stopped breathing altogether. Will slowly removed his shaking hands from the five-pound note.

Bessie, Queen Elizabeth, was not there. She was face down.

The kidney would go to Kay.

'No,' Kay cried. 'No!'

'Yes,' Georgie said, smiling, walking over to her sister's side of the table and hugging her gently. 'Yes, yes, yes, my beautiful twin.'

44

Will went to be tested the following day. In the first instance, all the nurse required was blood. So simple, after the long wait, to have a nurse extract liquid and place it in a small plastic bottle. Will watched as she labelled it. He'd always felt confident there'd be no problem. Now, though, he felt terrified. What if he was unsuitable? He willed the bottle of blood with his eyes: *You'd better do the right thing, pal.*

He went home that night and tried not to think about it. If his tissue type was compatible, there'd be many more tests to complete: general health, psychological well-being. He couldn't wait to get them done, to lie on a bench in hospital and count down from ten until he fell asleep. When he woke, Kay would be on the road to recovery. And he could look after her, and put the rest of his energies into helping Georgie.

Will, Kay and Georgie watched a goofy comedy that night. Huddled on the sofa eating crisps and linking hands, no one mentioned the test. Instead, they laughed till halfway through the movie, when it went seriously downhill, and went to their beds to not sleep.

*　　*　　*

'Will? It's Mr Jamieson.' The phone had woken him.

'Hello, yes.' Will's heart stopped.

'Can you come in to my office?

He didn't tell the girls. He showered and dressed as quickly as he could and drove to the hospital. How many of these tortuous waits would he have to endure, he wondered. How many would be bad news? Surely not all of them. Surely, this time, the news would be good.

*　　*　　*

Will sat down when asked to. Oh no, the guy was perching his bottom on the edge of the desk. It made him so nervous that sweat patches formed under his arms and on his chest. His hands were trembling.

'Your tissue type . . . '

'Yeah . . . ' Will asked. 'What?'

'It's not a match. Not even close to a match.'

Had he just heard those words? He had to repeat them to hear them properly. 'It's not even close to a match.' His voice was monotone.

'That's right.'

'Are you sure?' Will refused to let one sentence tie the noose. He didn't believe it yet. It couldn't be.

'I'm sure. In fact, Mr Marion, I don't know how to put this, but . . . '

'Put what?'

'After the results, I had a look through your file . . . '

'And?'

'I noticed a small detail in the profiles, something peculiar . . . it made me want to be sure.'

'Of what? Just tell me!'

'Your girls both have beautiful brown eyes.'

'I know that.'

'Your wife has blue eyes.'

'She does.'

'You have blue eyes.'

Will didn't say anything.

'Are you sure Cynthia is the mother?'

'Of course I'm sure. I saw them come out of her. What on earth are you saying here?'

'To be 100 per cent I did another test. A DNA test, rushed it through. Will . . . I don't know how to tell you this, but . . . '

'Just fucking say it.'

'Two blue-eyed parents cannot have

brown-eyed children.'

'What?'

'I'm sorry . . . it's genetically impossible. And the DNA test confirmed it. Mr Marion, I am so sorry, but you're not the girls' biological father.'

45

Heath had been in his new cell, in his new prison, for over one week. His engagement to Cynthia — and her newfound address in Glasgow — had pushed the transfer on a little. And now, here he was, sitting at the desk in his cell, chewing the end of his prison-issue biro. This letter had to be good. Perfect. If he convinced them, he'd be out within a week.

It wasn't just the freedom he could taste in his mouth, smell in the air, it was her, his Cynthia, waiting for him in this very same city. She'd wangled a housing-benefit flat in Govanhill. Nice old tenement, close to town, two bedrooms, furnished. It would be their marital home. They would put their instruments in one room and — yes! — get the band together again. They'd put a large double bed in the second, where they would do it as often and as imaginatively as possible.

Dear Sirs and Madams,

Heath began,

This year has been a really good one for me. I have been drug free. I have reunited with the love of my life, who I am going to marry. We are going to live at her new address in Govanhill, Glasgow. Most of all, I realise I have done wrong. I completed another victim awareness course last month and the man I killed did not have it coming even though he'd probably raped a woman and sold my heroin to nine-year-olds. And . . .

Oh, but it was no good. He'd written this kind of shite before, and they always turned him down. He needed something that would really grab them, let them know he had indeed changed and would not be a threat to the community.

He thought about some of his pals, come and gone. How did they convince the board? One had a dying mother who needed to be cared for — this had helped. One had a new baby. One had been rejected so often they just kind of had to let him out. One had done every course on offer three times over as well as joining the 'Garden Party' — i.e. the guys in green shirts who tend the three pot plants in the prison. Heath had the fiancée thing, but he had nothing else.

He needed to think about it. There must be

something he could write to convince them.

'Jones!' An officer had opened his cell door. 'Visitor.'

★ ★ ★

Heath waited for his name and table number to be called at the prison-side entrance to the visits hall. Beside him were eleven other inmates. He could already see Cynthia at table six. She looked out of it. Heath was jealous. He couldn't wait to get completely and utterly shitfaced.

'James, table three,' the officer said, and elderly sex offender James headed towards his loyal disbelieving brother at table three.

'MacMillan, table five!' Good-looking Preston MacMillan walked towards his crying mother. Heath watched this young boy closely. He was very pretty. A fish out of water. Not only that, but he stopped at Cynthia's table and spoke to her. She said something to him. How on earth did they know each other?

'Jones, table six,' the officer ordered and Heath waltzed over to Cynthia, eyeing pretty-boy MacMillan as he sat opposite her and took her hand in his.

'You know that guy?' Heath said, pointing to Preston.

'Aye,' she said. 'He's the private detective who brought me back from Egypt. He's a prick, Heath. In the hotel in Cairo, he got me to take my pants off then analysed me like some creepy pervert doctor. I don't like him.'

'I don't like him either,' Heath snarled, his brain ticking as much as a brain like his could.

On the table behind them, Preston McMillan sat with his mother wondering three things.

Who was that thug Cynthia Marion was visiting?

When would he see the new boy again? Came through prison reception the same time as Preston. Got changed in the dog box next to him. Had an interesting shaped back, like a swimmer's. After they'd changed into prison uniform, they'd both been escorted to the remand hall. The desk man sent Preston to a cell on the third flat and the new boy to one on the second. Would they meet at mealtime? Exercise, perhaps? What memento could he gather in this place? And where could he hide it?

Lastly, Preston wondered if his mother would ever shut up. *It's my fault, I've been a bad mother, I can't lose you as well! Oh, Preston, what I am to do?*

Tuning out his mother as much as possible,

he tried to hear what Cynthia was saying to the thug. This was all he managed:

HEATH: I don't care about anyone but you.

CYNTHIA: They looked so sick.

HEATH: And what about us? You think *we're* doing well?

★   ★   ★

As the prisoners were being escorted back to the halls some time later, Preston sidled up to Heath and said, 'So, you know Cynthia Marion?'

'What's it to you?' Heath said.

'Her daughter is a friend of mine. Sounds like you were talking about her.'

Heath stopped dead. 'You eary-wigging my conversation?'

'I suppose I was.'

'Tell you what. Sign up for hairdressing this afternoon. I'll fill you in on everything I know there.'

★   ★   ★

The hairdressing unit was a classroom opposite B Hall. Around twenty desks dotted the room, equipped with plastic-wigged heads. Implements were handed out under the strict supervision of the officer in charge

285

— scissors, combs, brushes, hairdryers, dye, bleach, clippers.

In his seat next to Heath, Preston listened as the officer tried to remain macho while teaching the basic skills of hairdressing.

'And how do you know my fiancée?' Heath asked Preston as they followed the instructions regarding washing and massaging the head.

'I don't really.'

'You didn't meet in a hotel in Cairo?'

'We met on a beach in Dahab.'

'And in a hotel in Cairo?'

'Listen, what's your name again?' Preston started.

'Holy shit,' Heath said midway through his attempt to give a number 1 to the blond wig before him. 'I've hurt myself here!' Heath had somehow managed to make his finger bleed.

'Wait there,' the officer said, worried by the blood that was spurting from Heath's finger. I'll get the first-aid kit.'

Unsupervised, Heath immediately grabbed Preston by the neck in a stranglehold, bashed his head facedown onto the table and put his knee on his back. He had the clippers in his other hand, which he held at Preston's head.

'You fucked my fiancée?' he said, turning the clippers on.

'No!' Preston said.

Heath shaved a neat line in the middle of Preston's head, from his neck all the way to his forehead.

'Tell me what you did.'

'She just asked me to touch it.'

Heath began to shave a second line to the left of the first.

'I don't like it when people lie.'

'I'm not lying.'

'You calling *her* a liar?'

A third line was completed. Heath liked his work. As always, it was meticulous, but it wasn't doing the job. He turned Preston around so he was facing him, held him firmly by the neck with one hand, grabbed the hair-dryer, prised open Preston's mouth with his fingers and placed the large round nozzle into his mouth, stretching it, filling it.

'You want to tell the truth now, you perverted prick?'

Preston couldn't speak. The hairdryer was in his mouth. He struggled. Why was no one doing anything to help? What was taking the officer so long?

Heath turned the hairdryer onto high.

Preston's legs wriggled as hot air blasted into his mouth and lungs. Tears streamed from his eyes.

Heath took the hairdryer out. Preston gasped. His tongue and throat were badly burnt.

'How about now? Anything come to mind?'

'She asked me to. I didn't want to! I didn't like it! I promise. I'm not a liar.'

'No, and I suffer from low self-esteem. We all do.' Several frightened-looking apprentice hairdressers laughed.

Heath put the dryer back in Preston's mouth, pushing it in further this time. Knee on his chest, he pinched Preston's nostrils with his fingers and turned it on high again.

Preston's legs wriggled for a while, then stopped. His face — and the thick bald stripe on his head — turned bright red, then grey, then blue. The men in the room watched, terrified. Was he dead? Should they do something? If they did, would they die too?

'How's that bleeding?' the officer said, returning to the room. Heath pulled the dryer from Preston's mouth just in time. He fell to the floor.

'What's wrong with him?' the officer asked, looking at Preston as he writhed and gasped on the ground, his hand over his scorched mouth.

'Cannae stand the sight of blood, the wee poof.'

Preston rolled around the floor, moaning.

'Get up, you fearty,' the officer said, before tending to Heath's cut finger.

46

It was like being told his head wasn't his. The news made everything inside him shudder. It had hit him, obviously, like a bowling ball-sized hailstone, but it didn't make any sense.

'That's ridiculous.'

'It's a fact. I can show you the test results.'

'No! I am their father. They're my girls. They even look like me. Look at this nose!' Will grabbed his nose angrily, wobbled it with his thumb and index finger. 'They have my nose!'

'I don't know what to say.'

'Have you heard Kay laugh? She laughs exactly the same way as me ... Kind of squeaky, ho-ho-ho!'

'Would you like a glass of water?'

'Would I like a glass of water? Listen to me! In bed, Georgie sleeps with one hand grasping her hair, like this.' Will pulled his fringe back with his right hand. Too hard. It would have hurt if he had any feeling. 'I do the same!'

'I'm going to pour you a whisky.' Mr Jamieson grabbed a bottle from the bottom drawer of his desk and poured a stiff one. Will took it, but didn't drink.

'They both like horror films. I like horror films.'

'Take a sip, Will.'

He took an autopilot sip. He wanted the doctor to take it back, take that stupid sentence, the one he'd said before, just grab it from the air and swallow it.

'I'm so sorry. I only wish I'd realised this sooner.'

Will placed the glass of whisky on the desk beside Mr Jamieson's still-perched bottom. He sat in silence for a moment, staring, then said, 'I'm going to leave now.' His legs shook as he stood up, and as he walked out the door, along the corridor, down the stairs, and into his car.

He sat in the car park for over an hour, staring at the pillar in front of him. Images flashed on the concrete.

The first time he held them in his arms at the same time. He had an itchy nose. Couldn't do anything about it.

That time at the window, when they were three, waiting for their mum to come back from the shops.

Kay's first concert. She had a flute solo. Will cried. Georgie got worried. 'Are you sad because she's bad at it, Dad?'

Georgie asking for a family movie, the three of them on the sofa, huddling, laughing.

All those years, all this time, it'd been the three of them. A team. Sometimes a crap one. Mostly, though, a good one.

But they did both look like him. Same hair colour, same nose. Kay had the same laugh. Georgie had the same sleep-pose, the same terrible organisational skills. Was it possible they'd taken on his characteristics purely by being around him? Nurture over nature?

All those years, and he was an impostor.

All those years, and he had been fathering someone else's children. Heath Jones's children, in all probability.

If they weren't his, then what was he? 'If I'm not their dad,' he sobbed, 'then what the hell am I?'

★   ★   ★

Someone was tapping on his window. Will wiped his eyes, looked up.

'You all right in there?' It was that chubby male nurse.

Will wound the window down. 'I'm fine.'

'You sure?'

'Yeah.'

'Okay, well take it easy, eh?' the nurse said.

Will shut the window as the nurse walked

towards the lift. He took his phone from his pocket. 'Georgie?'

'Hi, Dad, how'd it go?'

'Oh, fine. Nothing to report yet. I was wondering if Cynthia left her address when she came by.'

'Um, she didn't really. She said she was living in a hostel in Govanhill, but I think she's probably got a flat by now. Why? Is everything okay? Really no news?'

'None. Everything's great, darlin'. I'll see you soon.'

'Da — '

He didn't give her time to probe further.

⋆　⋆　⋆

There was only one hostel for homeless women in Govanhill. Will parked in front of it thirty minutes later.

'I'm looking for Cynthia Marion,' he said to the middle-aged barrel of laughs at the desk.

'She's not here. Got a flat.' The rude bastard didn't even bother looking Will in the eye.

'You know where?'

'None of your business.'

Will grabbed the man by his collar, pulled him towards him, and said, 'Tell me where

292

she fucking is, you fat prick.'

The flat, as it happened, was just around the corner from the hostel. There was no security lock on the main entrance, so Will walked in the close, which had graffiti all over the walls, and stinking rubbish all over the floor. The only door without a name on it was on the first floor. He knocked, then listened. No noise at first, then a groan, then footsteps and a door shutting, or opening, then another groan, then . . . 'Will? It's you!'

She was so high she could hardly stand. Her words slurred, her eyes protested against her attempts to open them. Will grabbed her arm and led her into the living room. The flat was a proper drugs den. No carpet. No heating. Junk and fags and drugs paraphernalia all over the place.

He sat her on the sofa, went to the kitchen, poured her a glass of water, came back into the living room and threw the water in her face.

'What the . . . ' She couldn't even finish the sentence. Her body wanted to lie down. Will wouldn't let her. He sat next to her and held her shoulders with his hands.

'Did you always know I wasn't the father?'

A hint of panic entered the half-closed slits of her eyes.

'Oh Will! Will Will Will . . . What did you say?'

'The girls aren't mine.'

Her head slumped towards her chest. She bounced it back up a second later, hearing what he'd said. 'Really? Wow. You know I wondered about that . . . '

'Is it Heath?'

'Of course it's Heath. He's my man, Will. Willy Willy. Can you tap me a tenner?'

'No, Cynthia.'

'I'll give you a blow job. That's very good value.' Her head slumped down again. This time, it took twice as long to lift back up and when she did her eyes remained shut. Will let go of her shoulders, laid her on the sofa, put a blanket over her and left.

47

Will couldn't see Heath until the next day and decided he couldn't see the girls until he had. How could he? They'd know it was bad news straight away. Not the full extent of it, but he couldn't face them. No, he needed to speak to Heath Jones first.

'Hey, guys,' he said into the answer phone, knowing they'd be at the hospital dialysing. 'I'm not going to be home tonight. There's soup in the fridge. Hope everything's okay. Everything's good here, just going to see Si in Edinburgh. Need a night out with the boys!'

He didn't go to Edinburgh. He booked into the Hilton in town, sat on the double bed, drank a half-bottle of whisky and passed out.

★   ★   ★

He hadn't eaten for twenty-four hours when he arrived in the visits room of the prison the following morning. His hands were shaking. His eyes were red and sore from crying. He put his clenched fists on the table in front of him and waited till the father of his children walked into the room.

'Well, look who it is.' Heath said, sitting down opposite him. 'The poofter.'

Will leant forward and spoke with a stern tone that had grown on him since using it for the first time with the arsehole at the homeless hostel. 'You are a useless piece of shit, Heath Jones, and I hate you. Before yesterday, the world was a much worse place with you in it and I'd have been glad if you were locked up in here for the rest of your life. But things have changed. Now, you have a purpose. Listen to what I'm going to say . . . Are you listening? I'm going to do you that favour I owe.'

Heath, taken aback by the change in the poofter said, 'Whatever.'

'You are the father of my daughters, Georgie and Kay. You have their genes. And you have the chance to save one of them.'

Heath burst out laughing. 'Well, how 'bout that!'

'I'm going to offer you a deal.'

'Oh yeah?'

'Yeah. I'll help you convince the parole board to let you out. Hell, I'll make them cry at how selfless and changed you are.'

'And . . . '

'Some tests, an operation, a rest in hospital. That's all.'

Hmm, Heath bit the nail of his thumb. He

296

imagined his first night of freedom, pure hedonism. He imagined seeing Cynthia again. He imagined having another year in this shithole. 'You got a pen?

Will gave the pen to Heath and began dictating the words he had composed in his head, being careful not to sound like someone with half a brain.

TO WHOM IT MAY CONCERN

I just found out I have two daughters. I didn't know they were mine till today and I am overjoyed. They are twins. They are sixteen years old. They have their whole lives ahead of them but they are very sick. Both of them are going to die from kidney disease unless I get out and help them. I want to do this to make up for all the bad I've done. I want to donate a kidney to Kay, because she is the sickest one. She is a very sweet girl. The man who looked after them is called Will Marion. He visited me and told me the news. I realise now that I have — and I want — responsibilities. I want to save Kay, but most of all, I want to be a father to both the girls, at long last. It gives me a purpose, a reason to live, a reason to be drug free and law abiding. I have been good this last year. I am getting old now. I want to change my life. I want to be a good person. I want to make up for what I done. I am being tested for compatibility immediately. I am also registering as a donor as soon as I have finished this letter in case anything happens to me before I get a chance to be a living donor. If you let me out, I will save a young girl. If you let me out, I will be in hospital for a while and I will not be able to offend. I do not want to anyway. I am a father now.

HEATH JONES

Will took the letter from Heath when he had finished and folded it. 'We're going to take this directly to the governor. She's agreed for us to go to the office now, get the tests organised and have you register as a donor online.'

Heath's expression changed to one of irritation. He quickly reverted to mock-cooperative and said, 'Fine. Let's go.'

Will had indeed organised these things with the governor. He'd phoned before the visit and explained the situation, asking if Heath could be tested for donor compatibility immediately. He also argued that prisons were dangerous places. 'If anything happens to him, he needs to have registered as a donor.' The governor, whose elderly mother was on dialysis, empathised and agreed to the last-minute visit. She had already arranged for the prison doctor to conduct the necessary tests and knew how to register online. 'Of course he has to comply to these things,' she'd said.

'Of course.'

Will helped Heath register online in the governor's office. The thug looked as sweet as he possibly could for the benefit of the woman who might help release him, even wiping a pretend tear from his eye as he talked of his newfound fatherhood. After they had finished he asked Will if he could have a photograph of the girls.

Will didn't want to give him one, but he also wondered if the sight of their beautiful faces might help Heath feel something, make sure he kept his word. 'You can have this one,' Will said, handing over a photograph of the girls on the beach in Arran. They were standing at the edge of the water, bare feet, jeans rolled up, arms around each other, smiling broadly.

Hmm, Will thought, taking one last look at the photograph as he handed it over, Georgie *is* smiling in that one.

'When does the board meet?' Will asked the governor.

'Tomorrow,' she said.

'And if he gets it?'

'Depends on us and on the criminal justice social-work service. If we have everything in place — all the conditions, like a suitable address, drugs counselling, anger management, whatever else might be considered necessary by the social workers and the Parole Tribunal, then it could be immediate. What I'll do is check if things are in place. If they are, all we need to do is get the licence drawn up immediately. Considering the urgency of the situation with your daughter, I could make sure this is done as quickly as possible. Of course, you mustn't get your hopes up. It's up to the Tribunal to decide. As you know, Heath, any breach of your life licence would mean an immediate recall to custody.'

'Of course, I understand.' Heath was still looking at the photograph. Will wanted to punch him in the face. How dare he look at the girls?

'In that case, Heath, if you are granted parole tomorrow and you're released immediately, could I come and collect you?' Will said.

'Oh, come on. Give me one night with my missus.'

'Right. One night. Then come to my house — you know where we live. You were a regular visitor there over sixteen years ago. Come to my house around midday.'

48

The Tribunal consisted of three members of the Parole Board for Scotland and a Chairman. Three of them knew Heath well as he had passed the punishment portion of his sentence several years ago and, since then, had repeatedly unimpressed them. His reports, letters and temper were notoriously poor. However, having read the social-work and prison-based reports, the board already felt differently about this year's application. They had, in fact, enjoyed a lengthy discussion before he arrived in the room. He'd completed as many courses as a prisoner possibly could, ranging from victim awareness to drugs counselling to anger management to hairdressing. He hadn't failed a drugs test and had worked in the joinery sheds and in the laundry. He'd even played a minor role in a play in the chapel. But it was his personal letter that clinched the deal.

'You are going to donate your kidney?' the younger of the two women said. She was around fifty-five, prim and proper.

'I am. I'm a perfect match, the doc says. I've got a letter here from a Mr Jamieson to say so. You want a look? It just arrived an hour ago.'

The four members of the panel took turns to read the letter Mr Jamieson had written that morning, the crux of which was that Heath's blood and tissue types were perfectly compatible with those of his twin daughters. Further tests would be required regarding general health and psychological well-being, but it was looking very positive indeed.

'So I want it done as soon as I can. I have two daughters I didn't know about. How about that, eh? Here I was, thinking I was a total waste of space, that the world was worse with me in it, and then I discover I'm a dad and that they need me, like in a life-or-death kind of way. I have to make up for lost time, be a father. Save a life. And of course, help with ... the one who'll still need a kidney ...'

He'd forgotten her name. Luckily, none of the decision makers noticed.

'Poor girls,' he said.

'And your address has been assessed as suitable by the social worker covering the Govanhill area,' the other woman said. She was around seventy. Had very short dyed brown hair and no eyebrows.

'That's right.' Heath was still wondering how Cynthia had managed to sit upright during the social worker's visit. 'We're going to get married.'

The board member who used to be a cop spoke next. Heath knew he was a cop because they'd assaulted each other on separate occasions, a year or so apart. The cop had come off worse. 'On the licence,' he said, 'we would want to add conditions.'

'Of course.' Heath tried to say *Sorry for breaking your nose* with his eyes.

'A condition to attend drugs counselling as directed by your supervising officer, as well as anger management and assistance with work or training.'

'Excellent,' Heath said. 'Soon as I've recovered I'd like to get a job. Buy presents for my daughters. Have a nice wedding.'

The vote was unanimous.

The prison worked at breakneck speed.

Heath would be released the following day.

49

I was delivering a note. It was a very lovely note. Alfred would like it. But he wasn't gonna get it. This note, it started like this:

Preston,

At 9 a.m. I woke up and went to the bathroom. I brushed my teeth for two minutes using an egg timer. I got in the shower. I got out. I dried myself. I got dressed in the bedroom. I went down-stairs. I had breakfast, crunchy-nut cornflakes and a glass of water. I watched the morning news in the living room for ten minutes. I rang the prison from the phone in the hall, arranged a visit with you and walked to the bus stop . . .

The letter was three pages long. I continued to write it on the bus, then finished it in the foyer of the prison. Would this suffice? If I sent him one each day, outlining the things he would see if he was watching me, would it be interesting enough? Would he read and re-read? There would be no secret messages, like the ones I dreamt my mother may have sent Heath, but the letter represented the kind of love I had yearned for. Difficult love, involving sacrifice and pain. Would Preston be my love story? I would know as soon as I saw him read my letter. If the answer was yes, then I wouldn't give a shit about Dad's tests, Kay getting the goods, me waiting, me living — or not.

I gave the butch woman and the effeminate man at the desk my ID, put my bag in the locker and followed a six-foot uniformed could-be model up the stairs and into the visits area.

Oh, Preston. Why was half his head bald? Without sunglasses, a full head of hair and a hiding place, I just didn't know him.

'How you doing?' I said, sitting opposite him. 'I brought you a letter.'

Preston was acting very strangely, like he had two tongues in his mouth. Don't know what the hell was wrong with the guy. He put out his hand and took the envelope. I waited for him to say something, or open it. Instead, he kept looking over at a young prisoner sitting at the table next to the door. Wouldn't take his eyes off him.

'Well, open it,' I said, so he did. Glanced at it for a tenth of a second and put it down.

'Who are you looking at?' I asked.

He could hardly speak. Something had happened to his mouth and throat. 'His name is Jason McVie.' He mumbled with difficulty, still not looking at me.

What was I thinking? Who was this guy?

'Jason McVie.' He didn't need to say it a second time. Once was enough for me to realise that he was not my love story. He'd already replaced me with an accessible young prisoner. He was just a good-looking stalker guy with a weirded-out mouth.

I paused, sighed, took the letter from him and put it in my pocket.

'I'm never going to fall in love with you, Preston,' I said.

50

Heath was released at 11 a.m. They handed him his allowance and belongings and escorted him to the front door.

Every time Heath got out, he rewarded himself with an extraordinary night before heading home to the missus. Things always happened on these nights. Good things. Fun things. Things he'd dreamt about in his cell bunk for however many months or years. This time, he had another element to look forward to. It excited him so much, the fact that the first chapter of this night would involve his newfound daughters, that he almost ran down the driveway and into the off-licence.

Celebratory bottle of whisky in hand, Heath caught the bus into town with three other new releases. The second bus he caught took forty minutes. By the time Heath arrived at the Marion residence, his bottle of whisky was empty.

He'd only been standing opposite the house for a minute when one of the girls came out with her keys and bag. So this was one of his daughters, didn't know which. Hmm, he thought. Where was she going? He walked fast so he could catch up with her. One step behind now. It made her look around. She checked him out then turned to the front again. She didn't know who he was at all.

He stood at the bus stop beside her, doing his own checking out. So this is what he could make with his most excellent sperm. Not bad. A bit gloomy and ill-looking, but not bad. He probably had at least five others out there somewhere. He wondered if they'd all have blonde hair and — if he did say so himself — a perfect physique.

On the bus, he took the seat behind her. She was a strange girl, stared blankly into space. When she got off in the city centre, he got off too.

She went into a bar in the Merchant City. Ah, the other one was there too. The same, but much prettier, softer, somehow. They sat together at a table in the corner of the bar and ordered two vodka and tonics from the waitress.

'You heard from Dad?' the pretty one said.

Dad. The word warmed Heath more than he expected. He was a dad! *Their* dad. These interesting girls were his daughters. He smiled and took a sip of his pint.

'No. Can't get hold of him,' the other one said. 'This is agony, isn't it? Must be a nightmare for you.'

'I thought I was going to fall in love today,' the gloomy one said.

'Who with?'

'That detective guy. He was following me. He's in prison now. I visited him first thing this morning.'

'Why's he in prison?'

'Stabbed a dealer.'

'Sounds perfect for you, G, blimey.'

'I know. I must have been going crazy. But I found him intriguing and elusive. And he was obsessed with me, I suppose. No one's ever been obsessed with me. It got to my ego. What am I like? Actually wanting a stalker!'

'How could we not go crazy, eh? God knows we need distractions. I feel awful all the time.'

So the gloomy one was Georgie, Heath thought. His kidney was for the pretty one, Kay. What would they think of him? Heath wondered. Would they like him? Would they buy him Father's Day presents?

'I know. Me too,' Georgie said.

'What do you think's gonna happen?' Kay asked.

Georgie took her hand, looked her in the eye and said, 'I reckon Dad'll be the business and you'll be brand new and I'll get one soon too and we'll go on holiday to Arran to celebrate!'

'Arran? I thought you hated Arran.'

'I thought I did too . . . '

'Excuse me,' Heath found himself standing awkwardly over their table, 'I couldn't help overhearing you like Arran. I have a second cousin who lives there.'

'Sorry, but we're having a private discussion,' Georgie said, a harsh look in her eye.

'Right,' Heath felt foolish for the first time since that procurator fiscal had said he was of below average intelligence. How had these girls managed to make him feel foolish? He felt his face heat up as he said, 'No problems' and returned to his seat.

'I have a confession,' Georgie said to Kay.

They hadn't even blinked as he left. Hadn't even had the decency to be polite. And all he wanted to do was get to know them a bit before he risked his life for one of them.

'What?' Kay asked.

'I've invited Graham for a drink.'

Kay looked horrified, then terrified, then jubilant.

'It's about bloody time you two got together. How long have you strung him along for? Look, there he is.'

A boy of around seventeen approached the table. He was a bit of a geek, a lovable type, the type Heath enjoyed knocking the living lovability out of.

Heath, now a little drunk, and angry at how they had dismissed him so coldly, listened to the chat about orchestras and yawned. Boring bastards. How'd he produced such boring bastards? Boring and cruel. Eventually, Kay and her boyfriend smiled, stood, and left. As they disappeared down the street, both Heath and Georgie saw them link hands. Gloomy Georgie girl smiled.

'You want a drink?' Heath asked her, standing over the table again.

'No thanks,' she said. She still had no idea who he was. Hadn't she seen him in the news? Maybe. He'd gained two stone since then, Heath supposed, and gotten older. He didn't look the same as he used to, but was he so different? He still had it, didn't he?

'Oh go on, just one. Your private conversation is over now, isn't it? We could have a chat,' he said.

'Just fuck off, will you?' she snapped.

'What did you say to me?' Heath said. He glared at her. This was her last chance. What she said next would determine her sister's future.

'I said fuck off, will you. And now I'm saying fuck off again. You stink, and you're a creep.'

312

Heath smiled, then laughed. To think he was going to help these arseholes (did he ever intend to, really?). What was so special about them? Why be attached to these particular sperm?

'What are you laughing at, weirdo?'

'Your sister's gonna be mad with you.'

'What?'

'You just sealed her fate.'

Georgie snarled then walked off. Probably assumed he was going to kill her there and then, rather than kill her sister there and then, indirectly.

What next? He hadn't enjoyed a good mugging in a while.

Three pints later and Heath had found his victim. A pretty lad who thought he was funny. Had three girls laughing at the bar, not realising it was only 'cause he was buying them drinks with all his pretty money. Heath followed him into the toilets. Nothing too fancy, he thought. Just a good simple:

Punch in the face

Kick in the balls

Punch in the face

Kick in the shins

Kick kick kick all over, on the floor.

Nice wallet. Nice and full, funny pretty guy. See how the girls at the bar like you now.

Heath took the wallet and left the

Merchant City bar glowing. Tonight was to be his last night in the UK. He'd leave tomorrow, with Cynthia of course. What next?

The prostitutes on Glasgow Green had either gotten older and uglier or he'd forgotten how talentless the city was. He bought two with some of the pretty boy's money, took them to a room in a cheap hotel and ordered them to:

Stand over me

Other one, you, this in your mouth

Now sit

Bend

Lick

Now just fucking lie there, bitches.

The relief in his balls was palpable. He felt happy. The only thing that'd make him happier was the love of his life, his wife-to-be, who would also have heroin waiting for him.

Ah.

★ ★ ★

The night was going well. Heath could really celebrate now. He didn't have to worry about some stupid promise to the poofter and the Parole Board. He got a taxi to Govanhill, walked up the shitey close and into the shitey flat she'd arranged for his release.

The door wasn't locked. He walked into the hall, into the lounge, and looked upon her. The love of his life. The exciting, dangerous, Cynthia.

'What the fuck have you done to yourself?' he asked. She was sprawled on the sofa, wearing a T-shirt and old grey underpants.

'Heath!' she said. 'Come here!'

He sat beside her. God, if she was the earner, they were screwed. He'd certainly have to put the price down.

'Did you get some gear?'

'I did. I did, honey. But you took so long! Where have you been?'

She'd fucking used all the gear.

'You used it all?'

'I'm sorry, honey. No, I didn't use it! Will took it. Where were you?'

'Will took it?'

'Yeah, he came this morning. Just took it. Said to tell you it was his insurance policy.'

'Open your eyes,' he said, grabbing her by the chin. 'Open your fucking eyes. How can you be sorry with your eyes closed?'

She tried very hard and they did open a little.

'I ask you to do one thing. One thing!' He tossed her head down, stood over her, took off his belt and began to hit her with it so that, eventually, she looked much sorrier.

51

Will checked with the governor and was told that Heath had been released that day. Tomorrow, then, they would meet. Till that time, he avoided the girls, staying in the hotel room, thinking. He called them so they wouldn't worry. Said the tests were still underway, no news yet, and that he was chilling with Si for a bit. They seemed happy for him. 'Have some fun!' Georgie said. 'We're going to try that too. We're going to head into town today. And tomorrow we're off to the beach.'

When they were out, Will visited Cynthia and took the heroin she had bought for Heath, knowing he would definitely come to the house as planned if this was the case. He then slipped into the house and rifled through an old box of videotapes until he found the one Cynthia had sent him all those years ago. In the loft was an old video player; he took that too. Wine in hand, he played the tape back in the hotel room.

The bathroom door is open. Will is taking a morning piss.

From a slightly hairy bum he squeezes a fart, as he usually does, interrupting the flow only slightly.

He's channel flicking. The babies are crying but he doesn't seem to notice . . .

He's saying, 'Hello, gorgeous!'

'What do you love about me?' she's asking from behind the lens.

'Um . . . ' he says. 'Everything.'

'No, what, exactly, specifically?' she asks.

'All of you. You're great,' he says.

He's turning the music down, then up a bit, then down a bit.

He's reading the arts section then nodding at it, then shaking his head at it . . .

'Hello, gorgeous,' he's saying.

'Talk to me,' she says. 'Tell me something.'

'Um . . . What would you like to talk about?' he replies. 'What would you like me to tell you?' . . .

Farting over the toilet again.

Channel flicking again . . .

How many times did he watch the film? A dozen? It was morning before he thought that maybe he should stop.

Morning before he realised that this was not him any more, this indecisive man, this scared, malleable piece of inaction.

317

Morning. The girls were going out today, they'd said, to the beach.

It was time to get dressed.

Time to act.

52

Kay and I arranged to meet Graham at the train station in town then head to Largs for a day of fresh air and no hospitals. I was a block from home when I remembered I'd forgotten my hospital-only phone. 'I'll run back and get it. Tell you what, meet you in town. I'll call when I'm on the train,' I said.

I knew there was something strange as soon as I opened the door. A bang coming from the office. Our mail strewn across the hallway. Dad was in Edinburgh with Si. Kay was on her way to the train station.

Someone was in the house.

I walked to the kitchen, quietly slid our largest knife from its wooden block and looked for the phone in the hall — the base was there, but the handset was missing. Where the hell was the phone? I tiptoed towards the office.

The door was open slightly. I peered in. The man from the pub yesterday was going through the papers on my father's desk.

I opened the door.

'Who are you?'

The huge lug turned towards me and

smiled. 'Oh, hi. Georgie, isn't it!'

'Who the fuck are you? And what are you doing in my house?'

He moved towards me, not scared by the knife in my hand. 'Now, now, why don't you just give me that,' he said.

I gripped the handle tightly. 'Get out of this house or I'll stab you.'

He kept moving towards me till the knife was actually touching his chest. 'You want to know who I am?'

'I want you to get out or I will push this into your heart.'

'My name is Heath Jones. And my heart is on the other side of my chest.'

My grip loosened. I moved it to the right. Heath Jones. My mother's lover. Of course. Under that flabby face was the tough murderer I'd seen in the newspaper article.

'What do you want?'

'I want my stuff.'

'What stuff?'

'Heroin. Drugs. The poofter stole it from your mummy. It's mine.'

I moved to the filing cabinet and looked in M for money. I grabbed the emergency envelope. Handing him the money, I said, 'I don't have drugs. This is the only money we have. Take it and go.'

He put the envelope in his pocket, but he

didn't go. He moved towards me again, smiling.

'I said go!'

'Now, now, no need to be so grumpy. Why are you so grumpy? Must come from your mother.'

'Get out!' I yelled, but my grip on the knife was loosening again. My hands were sweaty. I looked around the room — where was the phone? I needed to dial 999.

'You want me to tell you who I am, who I really am?'

'I don't give a fuck. I just want you to leave. NOW!'

'I'm your daddy, Georgie. You want to give Daddy a hug?'

'Get out,' I said, not listening to his nonsense.

'I don't think so,' he said, grabbing the knife so quickly I hardly realised he'd done it, then pushing me against the wall. The knife was now at my chest. His arm was pushing against my throat. I couldn't breathe. I kicked him as hard as I could but he didn't seem to feel it. I pulled his hair. Didn't stop him. I couldn't do it any more anyway. My brain couldn't get messages to my limbs. My eyes were bulging. He looked into them. He seemed to like the look of my bulging eyes.

'It's true. Isn't that funny? I'm your father.'

'Bullshit!' The word was barely audible. God, he was killing me. I was going to die. Everything in the room was blurry. I managed one more kick, right in the balls. He winced a little, but that was all.

'It's true, little Georgie. I just found out. I'm over the moon. I'm your daddy!'

'Bullshit!' I rasped again, knowing this was the last word I would be able to muster.

'It is true,' I heard, as everything started to go dark. But these two words didn't come from the guy who was killing me.

They came from the man standing in the doorway.

My *real* father.

Will Marion.

53

Will had never done anything bad in his whole life, bar the drunken pros and cons list in his notebook. Now, he was going to do something very bad indeed. He was going to kill a man.

What luck, that he'd retrieved his gun earlier that day, almost as an afterthought, having rifled through videos, knowing it was dangerous leaving it in the house with the girls and that he might need to have it on him to convince the prick to go along to the hospital.

What luck, having worked it all out the way he had.

Firearms: 8/10.

Luck, too, that he had researched how to use the gun (7a).

Had decided where to aim (7b), in the head, right temple.

Had determined to do it at home (7c).

Knew an ambulance would arrive within twenty-two minutes of the call.

Not so lucky that his daughter would witness it. But the bastard was trying to kill her. She had stopped moving.

Will moved towards Heath and placed the gun at his right temple. 'Let go of her now,' he said.

Heath did as he was told, dropping Georgie to the floor. She coughed, spluttered, sat up.

'Georgie, move out of the way,' Will said.

Will shouldn't have watched Georgie drag herself towards the door, hoping, praying that she was all right. He'd taken his eye off the ball, and Heath had grabbed the metal spike from the desk and tried to plunge it into his chest.

Will was quick, though. He shielded his chest with his left hand. The metal spike went right through it, stopping a millimetre short of his chest at the other end. Eighty or so defunct pieces of paper with lists of things to never do were now attached to the palm of Will's left hand.

Unfortunately, the shock had made him drop the gun from his other hand. The weapon hurtled across the room and under the sofa bed. Heath lunged to the floor, trying to reach it.

Will put the end of the spike on the ground, and pushed his hand down as hard as he could so it moved down the spike with a painfully slow, moist scrape. Eventually, his hand reached the floor and he pulled the metal base out. He shook the pieces of paper from his bloody hand — pieces of paper with lists that represented the man he used to be, the man who never did anything. Grabbing the spike at its base, he lunged towards Heath, who was still trying to reach the gun under the sofa bed. His head was at knee height. With an animal roar, Will plunged the ten-inch metal spike into Heath's right temple. He stopped when he realised what he'd done. Heath stopped too, placing his hand on his head, fumbling about. Had this really happened? Was there a stick in his head?

He looked at Will for confirmation. 'What is that? Is there something in my head? What have you done? Tell me what that is!'

Will's hand was no longer holding the base of the spike. He looked at the man kneeling before him, who was still very much alive. He looked at the spike. Two inches had disappeared into his thick skull.

'You know what I've done? I've started something . . . '

Will kicked Heath so he fell onto the floor on his side. Placing his foot on the base of the metal spike, he looked Heath in the eye and said, 'And now I'm going to finish it.' He pressed his foot on the base, pushed with all his might, eyes on Heath's, unflinching, until the spear exited the other temple and pressed into the underfelt of the carpet.

Why was he still breathing? Will thought, when he's impaled on a spike from temple to temple? *How was he still speaking?* Pleading, hand out to Georgie?

'*Georgie . . . Help me. Help your daddy. I'm your father. You're my own flesh and blood.*'

Georgie paused, watching the man weaken, watching him die. 'No you're not,' she said, reaching under the sofa for the gun and handing it to Will.

'This man is my father.'

★ ★ ★

There was no need for the gun. The spike had done the job. Heath stopped talking, expression faded from his eyes, blood dribbled from his mouth, his ears, his temples. A spasm, a gurgle, a loosening. He closed his eyes, and stopped breathing.

Will looked at his daughter. 'I'm sorry, Georgie. I'm sorry.'

Neither of them could avert their eyes from the dead man on the ground. What had Will done? He had killed someone.

Georgie leant down and checked Heath's pulse. Nothing. She touched his cheek, as if she hoped to feel something, some sadness at the loss of this man, but quickly retrieved her hand. She felt nothing. She stood and looked at Will, who seemed catatonic.

'You'll go to jail, Dad. I don't want you to go to jail,' Georgie said. He didn't respond. She grabbed his shoulders, shook them. 'Dad! Listen, you can't go to jail!'

Her words hurled him back to reality. He shook his head, clearing the debris.

'Right. I won't. Now listen to me. He killed himself,' Will said, putting the gun to one side.

'With that?' she said, looking at the spike. 'That's ridiculous.'

'No,' Will said, standing over Heath's dead head and grabbing the base of the spike. It exited the temple with a sucking hiss. Will picked up the gun, wiped it clean with his T-shirt and placed it in Heath's hand. Turning to Georgie, he said, 'Don't look. Leave!'

Georgie didn't move. What could be worse than what she'd already seen?

'I said OUT! Now, Georgie!'

She backed out of the room, shut the door, slid down behind it, her head in her hands.

A moment later, Will placed Heath's body on its side on the blood-soaked carpet, positioned the gun against his right temple, checking the angle was correct and would make the same journey as the spike. He took a deep breath and pressed Heath's fingers hard against the trigger.

The noise made Georgie jump, and then scream, and then sob.

* * *

It was a few minutes later when Will tried to open the office door. 'Georgie, let me out. Move away from the door!'

She crawled forward so her father could get out of the office. Will opened the door and kneeled in front of her.

'G, it's okay. Keep your cool. I'm going to clean up. You're going to write a suicide note.'

'But . . . How? I don't know his handwriting.'

Will handed her Heath's iPhone. 'This was in his pocket. Do a text. Don't make it too clever. Clean your fingerprints after. Rub his fingers with it, send it to Mr Jamieson. I've put the number in his contacts. You understand? Tell the doctors to get here. Then put it next to him and wash yourself. Can you do that?'

'I can.'

'When you have, we'll get hold of Kay.'

54

'Bessie up or down?' Will said, palm down on the new dining table in their recently renovated kitchen. All three looked different. There was no yellow in the girls; no sadness in Will. Kay's hair was several inches longer. Georgie had dyed hers black.

'Down,' Georgie said.

Will lifted his hand slowly. Lizzie was indeed down.

'Ha!' Georgie said.

'So where do you want to go?' Will asked.

'You know where? To the sofa. I want the three of us to watch your new film and eat crisps . . . for a whole week!'

'Its not ready! It's uncut!' Will said.

'Don't care. Wanna see it,' Georgie said.

It was a deal.

★   ★   ★

It had been such very good news, all those months ago, because Heath Jones had died. Will had cleaned fingerprints and bloodstains thoroughly. He had shot

329

accurately. The police did not suspect foul play and had escorted him to the hospital to be with his girls as the operations took place.

And his darling Georgie had written the perfect goodbye, the heart-wrenching note for which Will had always yearned.

TO MR JAMIESON

Ive failed. Ive missed the real thing. Ive never loved. Ive been a bad father.

I never read them stories, hugged them when they missed their mum, didn't take them to school, watch them play netball, help them with their homework, cheer them up whenever they were down. I never loved them different but equal. I haven't sat next to them at the kidney machine for hours on end, week after week as they wait to die. Ive not been that man. Ive been a bad man. Ive never done anything that wasn't selfish. Never loved. It's time for me to make up for it. So this is my love story, my sacrifice, my gift. Im sorry to do this in front of anyone, but I need to make sure they go to the hospital with my body, pronto. Please, please,

make sure both *my* girls get what they
need from me.

At the bottom it was signed:

Heath Jones

Father

THE END

We do hope that you have enjoyed reading this large print book.

Did you know that all of our titles are available for purchase?

We publish a wide range of high quality large print books including:
Romances, Mysteries, Classics
General Fiction
Non Fiction and Westerns

Special interest titles available in large print are:
The Little Oxford Dictionary
Music Book
Song Book
Hymn Book
Service Book

Also available from us courtesy of Oxford University Press:
Young Readers' Dictionary
(large print edition)
Young Readers' Thesaurus
(large print edition)

For further information or a free brochure, please contact us at:
Ulverscroft Large Print Books Ltd.,
The Green, Bradgate Road, Anstey,
Leicester, LE7 7FU, England.
Tel: (00 44) 0116 236 4325
Fax: (00 44) 0116 234 0205

Other titles published by
The House of Ulverscroft:

DEAD LOVELY

Helen FitzGerald

Krissie and Sarah have been best friends since they were children. While Sarah has been married to Kyle since university, trying — unsuccessfully — to have a baby, Krissie is carefree and single . . . But then Krissie accidentally becomes pregnant following a dalliance in a Tenerife toilet cubicle. For Sarah, who's long been trying to conceive, Krissie's unplanned pregnancy seems unfair. Things between them get worse during a walking holiday round Loch Lomond with Kyle. At first the days pass blissfully as the three friends laugh, chat and reminisce. But one night friendship turns to betrayal, and betrayal turns to murder . . .

MR MICAWBER DOWN UNDER

David Barry

The ever optimistic Mr Micawber bids a fond farewell to David Copperfield, taking his family to Australia, confident their lives will change for the better. However, florid language and optimism is not enough to survive the brash life of Melbourne in 1855. Visits from the bailiffs, rent arrears, and his daughter Emma's betrothal to his landlord's son, all complicate Micawber's life. However, when his son Wilkins introduces a young man with an ambiguous past, who also has designs on Emma, it becomes even more tangled. Micawber turns detective, but will the mystery he uncovers threaten even his optimism and integrity?

JUST ANOTHER DAY

Patricia Fawcett

Is Francesca making a mistake when she decides to buy her childhood home in Devon? Or could this help her to come to terms with something that has haunted her for years? Can she ever be rid of the guilt she feels for the accident to her brother, for which she feels responsible? Meanwhile, her meeting with her old friend Izzy brings things to a head, for she was present that day and knows the truth. But can Izzy and Gareth, the new man in Francesca's life, help her find a way to forgive herself at last and move on?

THIS BEAUTIFUL LIFE

Helen Schulman

The Bergamots' move up to the city goes well. Richard gets consumed by his new job and Liz, having given up her career, plays mother to six-year-old Coco and fifteen-year-old Jake. But when Jake, unthinkingly, forwards a sexually explicit email attachment sent to him by a young girl, the Bergamots' comfortable middle-class existence is over. Within hours, the video clip is all over Jake's school, the city — and the internet. Facing impossible choices, what Richard and Liz do next risks destroying everything: their marriage, their daughter, their place in the community and Jake — the child they have set out to protect.